THE DAY THAT <u>SHIT</u> CHANGED

DERRICK JACKSON

Printed in the United States of America

Street Credibility Publishing
P.O Box 14523
Cincinnati, Ohio 45250
Website: www.streetcredibilitypublishing.com

Street Credibility is a federally Registered trademark
Library of Congress Control Number: 2023919547
ISBN: 979-8-9888270-0-9 (Paperback)
ISBN: 979-8-9888270-1-6 (eBook)

Editing by Parker Hansen
Cover design by Prescribe Digital

Published by Street Credibility Publishing

DEDICATION

I dedicate this book to Virginia Jackson and Stephanie Jackson because they stood with me in the fire when nobody else would and I love you with everything I have in me. And to my kids Damir, Dy'year and Shy'fear you also have made sacrifices and for if, whatever is mine is yours, don't never forget how much I love you.

It was January 12, 1984, the day I came into this world, I fought through 2,000 other sperm to get here, Early in the morning at UC Hospital in the sweet state of Ohio, Cincinnati, Ohio, born and raised in the roughest part. Today was supposed to be a special day, a beautiful moment between two people, sharing a bond like no other. My beginning was different, my situation was like most, I came in this world another fatherless child. My mother Renee Nicole Wright was 16 years old, a child, having a child of her own. My grandmother was present, she stood in the place my father should have been, she is a strong black woman, who came from the south, deep down in Dickie Mills Alabama. She moved to Cincinnati when she was young, she had five kids, my mother being the only girl, made my momma tough as nails, my grandmother did all she could do to keep her family together and shit in line. We all grew up together in the same household and like any low income household it had its ups and downs. It built me physically and mentally, we had to fight for our bacon. My uncle Pete, was one of my favorite uncles, but he got messed up really bad on dope, and he would steal any and everything that wasn't nailed down. He broke a lot of the family trust, I got to see firsthand, just what addiction can do, and that shit tears families apart. I was a very curious child coming up, in other words, I stayed in some shit. I kept my eyes open up to everything around me. When my uncle Pete was gone, I would sneak into his room, and play with his dirty needles and looking at porno books, by the age of 3 years old sex, money, and drugs was all around me. To the sight of a child everything looks or is cool until you are told different. Just a few years later, my momma moved out of my grandmother house, it was time for her to do the things that she wanted, in her journey for love, the screams would come through the walls, I remember feeling helpless as I beat on the door in attempt to help her, ready to take on my role as a man, I only wanted to stop her pain and when I couldn't, I would cry myself to sleep. It didn't take long to learn the difference between pleasure and pain, especially after I drilled a hole in the wall, so I could watch, it was a crazy way to learn about pressure and pain. Being in the streets took away my innocents, I looked for love in all the wrong places. I always felt like my life was missing a father, I always wondered what it would be like to have one, every time I asked my mother about my father, she would tell me, fuck that worthless mother fucker, and she would send me away, with all my answers, unanswered, my grandmother went from street to church real quick, by my mother having to work all the time, she would send me to my grandmother house to keep me off the streets, but it didn't work, when I could, I would hit the streets, and the rest of the week was in the church with my grandmother, praising the lord, listening to the preacher break down the knowledge between good and evil, dough I wasn't into cutting a rug or chasing out demons, I built a strong faith for God, but yet and still, I made the streets my home, yea, the street life is the life that I chose, my uncle Pat use to tell me, as long as your game is strong, you'll always land on your feet. I watched my uncle Pat, put his foot in the game, I mean hitting the ground hard, moving packs, and I knew, even dough he tried his best to hide it from me, but I knew. His run didn't last too long, he got spooked after they killed his boy Kirk, he was never the same, after that, they caught him slipping on his porch on a hot summer day, they slipped out of the alley next to his house and put his brains in his lap. It was tragic, I felt so sorry for my uncle Pat, he didn't get out the bed for weeks, and when he did, he was done with any and everything that has something to do with the streets, I learned early on in life, you have to be built a certain way, to have your hand in these streets, my momma always told me, you would rather lose a hand, then your mother fucking life, so don't go all in on any one move, and if you lose a hand, maybe now, you will respect the other one. I always thought, now, why would I even risk losing a hand in the first place. When I jumped in the game, I was just turning 9 years old. I learned everything I know from the junkies; they became like a second family to me in the streets. One I ran across was named May-so, now May-so wasn't like all the other junkies, at one point of time, he was a well-known drug lord, a real kingpin who ran the streets, he got caught up in his love for the women, and one of them laced his joint with crack cocaine and he hasn't been right ever since, I got a lot of love for the dude, he has been the first and only father figure, not only who I could look up too but in my life, all my game, comes from him, he taught me how to sale dope with no dope. He has always been a real smooth dude; he has always been able to talk anybody out of anything he wants. May-so got me my first gun, right after he handed it to me, he said.

Now son the rest is up to you.

And he was right, it was up to me, I knew now that I was in the streets, it was only a matter of time, those same streets, was gone come for me and I had to be ready, I started off all wrong, I lead with trust and the streets is the total opposite, you're not supposed to trust no one. This game has never spared me even once. One day I was sitting out on the comer, in front of the store Jet-In, I had been putting in work all day, chasing down carts and running up on junkies, trying to get my pack off as fast as I can. I kept my dope stashed in the alley next to the store, just in case the police want to decide to try to pocket check a young nigga, where I'm from, no matter how old you are, they still a lock your ass up, if you caught slipping. Shit was moving fast, I re-upped about three times already, so I was having a great day. Out of nowhere, comes this fast talking junkie goes by the name of Sunny, this dude walked around with an itch and no matter what, his job was to try to get over at all cost.

What's up Lil Wright, make it right for me baby! Yea, if your money right, I got you.

Sunny was the type you don't even move for, unless, you see the money first.

I said, I'll make it right as long as the money is right, now let me see the money.

Sunny came out his pocket, with a balled up hundred-dollar bill to show Wright then he quickly placed it back in his pocket.

I got a hundred for you if you make it right, now it's your turn, show me something, said Sunny.

I wanted that hundred bad, it would not only put me on a fast track to re-up again, but I also knew I was due for a break, I been out here all day, I knew it was only a matter of time, my momma would be looking for me, shit probably even send a search team out looking for my ass. I walked into the alley to my stash spot, Sunny not far from behind. As I look back, I could see his eyes all over me, checking my every move.

Damn Sunny watch my back and not my pack.

He had a hungry look in his eyes, a look that carried no soul. His eyes were blood shot red. His face was sunk in and you can tell he was losing weight more and more every day because his clothes was real dirty and barely holding on. His shoes were like they was being held together by one string and once it popped he would be walking with bear feet on concrete. I grabbed my pack and sorted out piece by piece in my hands.

Come on Sunny, grab those pieces right there, you want a hundred right I asked.

Sunny made a motion to go in his pocket so I watched his every move. Sunny looked up with one quick motion before he spoke.

Shit, Lil Wright the police is coming, watch out!

When I looked up to see which direction the police were coming from, Sunny popped my hand up in the air and punched me square in the face, sending the dope flying everywhere and knocking me out cold. When I woke up, I was sore and confused on what happened. I didn't have a clue on where I was, my pockets were turned inside out. Sunny had ran off with everything I had. All the money, dope, and my pride to go along with it. I picked myself off the ground and started my walk home. When I walked into the house I was greeted by my mother at the front door. She was angry, one, because I have not been home all day and two, my face was swollen like I had got into a car wreck.

Where the fuck have you been and what the hell happen to your face.

Tears began to flow down my face and for the first time I was lost for words. I went in for a hug and then (smack).

A hand came across my face and I fell to the floor. I lifted my head, eyes wide.

Stand the fuck up like a man, only bitches can catch a wet face on they knees. Now go take care of your business, if somebody put they hands on you, you better fight them back, don't run in this house looking for me to help you, I'm gone beat your ass.

I got up off the floor angry, shaking, and crying wildly. I just knew whatever I was looking for out of that moment, I didn't get it. I went upstairs headed to my room, it was when I walked past the bathroom, I caught a glimpse of myself in the mirror, which stopped me dead in my tracks. I walked back to the bathroom and looked directly in the mirror and I couldn't believe the face that was staring back at me. The anger began to build more and more. I went to my room into my hiding spot to get my chrome 380 that May-so got me. In my heart I always wish I didn't have to use it, and to tell you the truth, I still was holding on to that hope that I don't. my mind began to run wild, maybe I could just scare him and he will give me my stuff back and maybe I won't have to pull the gun out at all and we can talk about everything. At that moment I could not shut my momma's words out of my head no matter how much I try to talk myself out of it. I could hear her say only bitches have wet faces on they knees, now go take care of your business. I wiped whatever tears I had left away. In my heart I knew I couldn't let him get away with what he done to me. I wouldn't have any respect in the streets. May-so always told me, it takes respect to make money. He just never told me I was going to have to take my respect from the ones who wasn't willingly to give. I tucked the 380 in my pants and threw my shirt over it, to conceal it out of view. I grabbed my CD player and threw 2pac inside and put my ambition as a rider on repeat as I made my way out the door. I walked, what felt like for hours, from Elm Street to Race Street, then Main Street. I went to every bar on every corner, Martins, was one of the spots where all the licks would go to get high and catch a drink. I didn't stick around any place for too long because I didn't want to make a scene or him to make one for that matter, the less people involved the better. I took my walk down to sweet Sandy house because that was the next best place I always could get my pack off. Sometimes I would sneak out the house late at night and go to sweet Sandy's and get top dollar for whatever I had. There aren't too many got the heart to do what they call the grave yard shift, it's nothing to get robbed and killed at them hours and nobody would never know who did it, you would be just another cold case. Now back to sweet Sandy, she is one of the sweetest woman I know, she would cook for me, pull me in on the big licks, and keep me up on what's going on in the streets, especially if I haven't been around in a while. I always wondered how she knew so much, when she never left the house. Sweet Sandy house was also a place for people to smoke crack you wouldn't even think smoke. One time I ran into my big cousin Sharon and we both was surprised to see each other. She made me promise to keep what she does a secret and in return, she taught me how to cook up dope from a pop can to a Pyrex, which took my money to a whole another level. But I do have to admit, it did make the family gatherings odd. I talked to sweet Sandy for a hot second and she told me she seen Sunny earlier and he was high as hell and buying up all the dope he could find. She searched my eyes for details but I just lied and said I wanted in on the money I heard he hit big and I wanted in, in my heart I could feel she knew because today there was no smiles, no laughs, just straight up business, in the air. I headed back out the door and back on to the street. I began to tire myself out on my search for sunny so I started my way back down Elm Street to grab something to eat at my grandmother's house, as I walked past an alley that was right next door to her building. I saw a figure sitting in the back alley alone, so I took a step back just to focus my eyes, to make sure if it was him or not and it was. I stepped back, then headed real slow down the alley, in my mind I was trying to figure out how I'm going to put my words together or just what I'm going to say.

My legs were shaking out of control, it almost felt like the ground was moving under my feet. Sunny was sitting down stuffing piece after piece into his pipe not even paying attention to my slow walk down approach.

What's up Sunny, I need to holla at you.

When Sunny looked up he had one of the evilest smiles on his face that I have ever seen. Naw Lil Wright you don't need to holla at me our business is threw.

Sunny the shit you did aren't right man and for real I thought we was cool.

Lol, we are cool Lil Wright, it's just part of the game we play Lol, today's game you snooze you lose, now get the fuck away from here before you make me mad, I'm trying to enjoy my high.

Sunny bro I am not leaving without my shit!

A, A, A, boy don't you mean my shit! Now listen to me if you don't get the fuck out of here, I'm gone knock your ass out again.

As I turn to walk away I could hear my momma voice loud and clear oncG again (take care of your business) I turned back around, chrome 380 in hand, shaking, hoping the sight of the gun would change the mood.

Ok Lil Wright, you want some attention, now you got it. You come down on me blowing up the spot, fucking with my high wit that pretty Lil thing you got in your hands there, the only thing I'm wondering, is you, gone, pop it!

Listen Sunny I don't want to but if I have to then I will!

Sunny started moving faster towards me as almost to a full sprint Then you have to because you ain't taking nothing from me (Pow Pow).

I squeezed the trigger sending two shots to explode into Sunny stomach and chest, the impact brought him to his knees. I ran up on him and went straight for his pockets looking for something to put the pieces of my life back together, that he stuffed in his pipe piece by piece for hours at a time. With my hands searching through his pockets we locked eyes and then he grabbed me with what it felt like all the strength he had left. Blood flowed out his mouth and down his chest as he looked like he wanted to share more words. I released my hand from his pocket and brought it to his neck and began to beat him over the head until he released his grab. I got up, my mind began to flip, I knew there was no turning back now and I couldn't let him live, so I stood over him and started firing all into his face until I emptied the whole clip. Reality set in really quick and I began to panic. I ran into my grandmother's house, threw all my clothes into a garbage bag and from the thought of what I just did, made me weak to my stomach, it began to turn in knots. I could feel the sweat pouring down my face and whatever was holding my stomach in place before, all bats were off now, everything from the bottom of my gut came out uncontrollably, I made a trail all the way to the toilet and prayed to it religiously. From the toilet I could hear the sirens getting closer and closer I knew I had to get up and get myself together before I brought any attention to myself. My head was spinning like crazy, I just hope tomorrow can be a start to a better day.

I woke up the next morning to the smell of grandma's famous pancakes, bacon, and egg's she always knew how to throw down, with a hand I only wished, I could have some day. I mean her shit is so good, it should be in a restaurant somewhere. I climbed out the bed still feeling tired and beat down from yesterday, Sunny really did have a nice right hand, but the key word for today, is had, that shit stops with me. I wasn't able to get no sleep, I was truly in my feelings, stuck between sorrow and paranoia but through it all I still couldn't find regret. What was done, had to be done, and believe me if I had to do it again, then I would do it again. I walked down the stairs not finding too much out of place. My uncle Pat was speed eating so he can hurry up and catch that bus for work. My uncle Coosa was rocking hard to the music in his favorite chair, not paying anybody no attention and grandma was on the phone probably talking to one of her sisters or brothers, she got like twelve of them, but I did key in on her conversation because she was talking about what happen yesterday.

Yeah girl, somebody got killed right outside my house yesterday, aw huh lit his ass up out there, it's been on the news all morning, they did that shit in board daylight, and I'm surprise, didn't nobody see shit.

The news came on right in the middle of her conversation, I hurried to turn it up.

News: yesterday a man named Sunny Mitchell was gunned down in an alley on Elm Street around 6:30 in the evening, police say that it was a drug related crime due to some of the evidence that were collected on the scene at this moment there are no suspects but if any one has any information please call crime stoppers at 513 348-2711.

Lamar, Lamar, boy you know you hear me! I snapped out of my thoughts.

Your momma mad as hell you didn't check in with her last night, but I told her you were sick all that damn throw up you had all over the place, do you feel any better?

Yes, ma'am I think I just at something bad that didn't agree with my stomach.

I headed back upstairs to get ready for my day but before I left I pulled out the chrome 380, wiped it down and reloaded it, I could feel this power all of a sudden, a greed for more blood was running through my veins, with it, it made me feel untouchable, so instead of putting it away, I placed it on my waist.

I went back to the streets but not in full force, I had to lay low, I didn't need people talking, putting my name in shit, I didn't need the police catching wind of it, then my life would be over for me, just like that, over a little reward money. I knew to keep my mouth shut but I was still holding on to a dangerous thing. The murder weapon, I couldn't just sale it because it would lead a trail back to me and plus I needed money, I was broke and it would take me forever to get back with the change that I had, so the next best thing would be to bust a move. I knew of this big time dope boy by the name of Money Mo, he took me under his wing a little bit, fronted me some dope, but would charge me some crazy high prices. I been in the streets for a while so I knew the game, he was trying to run on me, but when you broke and hungry, you will take anything you can get. Well after I got my money right, I didn't want to be fronted anything no more, I came with cash up front, no more handouts, no more treating me less than a man because I needed a little help, I had my own money so I thought maybe he would treat me like an equal. He sold me an ounce of bullshit, it looked like dope, cook like dope, but ain't no dope in it. I called him over and over but he never answered the phone. That crushed me, the friendship I thought we had was over, now I just had to wait for the right time to get my revenge. In this game there is no room for mistakes and Money Mo made more than a couple. I knew his route, every Friday I would ride with Money Mo to meet his connect, he would pick up a couple of bricks, then we would slide to the storage unit to switch cars, we would ride to different spots to pick up money, he would throw me a little something and drop me off on the block. Money Mo was a drinker and a smoker and would forget his life if he wasn't living it. Never mix business with pleasure, in the mix of everything, he showed me all his spots, even where he laid his head every night. When you high, you think in your mind that you are on point but in reality, you expose yourself in every step. When Money Mo wasn't paying attention I stole his storage key off his key chain and made a copy, then put it back before he even knew it was gone, I knew it was a matter of time before he would cross me, in truth, nothing last forever, I just had to wait for the right time to make my move and the right time was when I started running with this low down dirty dude by the name of skep Dollar, in the streets, his name rings bells. He would do any and everything for some money. He wasn't the type you can turn your back on because if you did, it would only take seconds to lose your life. I ran with Dollar on a couple moves, he would always get the bigger cut, and that didn't matter to me, I was mainly there for the game, not the money. In these last couple weeks Dollar been pushing me to run into different moves blind.

Come on Lil Wright, we need to bust a move, I got a couple Lil niggas I seen hitting licks around the corner.

Naw man, that ain't enough cheese for the both of us and plus that's only gone bring more beef we don't need, I said.

Fuck these niggas, when it comes to this money anybody can get it.

I let my next words be carefully said, Dollar was an older guy then me so he liked to push his bully around, plus he lacked common sense and emotion, I figured the only way to put him on ice is to lead him to a bigger gold.

Look Dollar, forget those dudes, I got a better move Ok, I'm listening Dollar said.

I got this move I been working on, he more than a little up in the game, he been moving bricks all around the city for a while now, so I know he has a lot of money stashed away, I can take you where he lays his head at.

O yeah, so let's hit that spot tonight, we ain't got to wait no longer, as long as you got the address, then we there, Dollar said.

Now hold on Dollar, it isn't just that simple, this guy is well known around the city and he has the type of money that can start a world war 3.

You sound like you scared or something Lil homie Dollar said.

Hell Naw, I am not scared, it's just if we don't do this the right way, we would have money on our head and we can have beef coming from any and every way we turn.

Man fuck that nigga, for the right money I'll, I'll kill that mafucka myself, from the way you talking, this one lick can set me up, I mean us up for life, we can pull out the big guns on this one.

Naw Dollar wait, I got a couple of guns we can use fresh out the box, I just bought them from a guy coming from Kentucky, he traded me some dope for them I said.

I hear you Lil Wright, but if we go in there with a couple AK's we can shut the party down.

Yeah but it's gone draw a lot of attention to us, there isn't no telling who will be looking out their windows and if I think he got what I think he got, it will be too much to carry so we need to travel light.

For the first time ever, I could see him starting to listen to me and that was something I needed the most, I didn't need him running around playing cowboy with something as serious as this.

So when do we move on this thing, Lil Wright?

Fridays, he always goes to meet his connect, so I think the best time to catch him would be on Thursday I said.

Dollar shot Lil Wright a confused look.

Why wouldn't we hit him on Friday so we can catch him with all the drugs and make twice as much money? Dollar said.

Dollar, we're not known for moving big weight on the streets, so after something happen to him, it wouldn't be hard to put the pieces together. We want all money and nothing else, but if we do come across a little dope, we grab it but we need to move it slow on a low level hustler style, so we don't draw no attention to us.

Low level hustler, fuck that shit, when I get my shit I'm gone do what I want, I am not worried about no attention, when these hoes see me with his bag they gone give this dick some real personal attention Lol, something I know, you don't know about.

You don't know shit, but on some real shit, we gone move at night, late, so we can catch him while he sleeping I said.

Sound like a plan to me, just hit me up when you ready said Dollar.

After me and Dollar had our little conversation, we split up, I couldn't hang around with him for too long, isn't no telling what would happen, he already been shot three times and the word is people already had money en his head and that's been known for a while now but aren't nobody stepped to the plate to come get it, that don't mean somebody won't, it just means the right man haven't stepped up, one crazy enough to gamble with life and love the taste of death. I started on my way home, wheels turning in my mind trying to put all the pieces together for when me and Dollar bust this move, I took the long way home playing everything out in my mind, bothered by the what ifs and how could I's, not paying attention to what's going on around me, all of a sudden I was snatched off my feet and threw into a wall.

Lil Wright what the fuck is up.

I had to adjust my eyes and when they came clear, it was May-so.

May-so, what the fuck, why you pushing up all on me?

You thought I wasn't going to find out? You thought I wouldn't be able to put it together.

The look in his eyes spelled out a mix of sadness and anger, it wasn't clear to me just what he was talking about just yet.

May-so what are you talking about, I tell you everything man!

May-so loosen his grip and released me back on my feet, a strong look of disappointment covered his face.

Yeah, you tell me everything, besides the fact that you killed Sunny!

My heart instantly dropped into my stomach, how do he know? Who told him? How did he find out? Did somebody see me? I became lost for words and before I could even speak, he corrected me, May-so I, I, i.

Lil Wright don't even do it, I know you better then you know yourself, and I didn't know what you did until just now!

What do you mean, I don't understand, you did all of that like you knew and for some time now!

He walked in front of me and got down on one knee, looking me eye to eye, his tone in his voice had soften, turning from anger to true concern.

You failed the test, May-so said.

The one where pressures are being applied, all it takes is for the cops to pick you up for questioning and your face would tell everything, Lil Wright you slipping and I bet you still got the damn gun, don't you?

I could no longer hold my eye contact, I dropped my head, May-so had read me like a book, he looked deep into my soul because my window's was wide open, I felt small and looked my age at that moment, everything he said was true but a part of me still felt like it was more to the story, like it's something that he is not telling me, I just know I had to get a head of everything before everything finds and gets behind me, tears began to flow down my face.

Oh no, no, no, you can wipe them tears away, you lost your position as a child as soon as you pulled that trigger, I'm staring in the face of a grown man now and what you do from this point about this situation is your business.

He stood up straight before I could say one word, he turned his back on me and walked away, I wiped my face and called his name over and over again but he never turned back around, he just kept walking.

When I got home, I put a lot of thought into what May-so had said and he was right, I would be foolish if I didn't get on point, the police can snatch me up at any time and I have to be stone faced, emotionless, and clear of any evidence that could lead me to that homicide but first I have to stay focused on the lick with Skep Dollar, yeah cleaning up my hand is more important but on the other hand this move can change my life, so I called Skep Dollar.

Ring, Ring, Ring, Dollar: a yo what's up.

Lil Wright: what's good the me bro.

Dollar: what's up what's good this Lil Wright?

Lil Wright: yeah this me, I was calling to see if we still on to hit that move tonight? The time is right,

Dollar: bro don't call me with no stupid ass questions like that Lil bro, you already know that I'm down, the only question is what time is we leaving?

Lil Wright: come pick me up around 1:00 am we should pull up like around 2:00am they should be good and sleep about time we make a move on them.

Dollar: alright bet, I'll holla at you in a minute.

We pulled up to the house, right across the street where we could watch from a distant, Skep Dollar was acting different, like he had a whole lot on his mind, usually he is a man of many words, tonight on the ride over he never said one.

What's up Lil Wright, you ready to do this move? Yeah, I said.

You brought the guns for us right?

Yeah, you know I did, everything is all good, I said.

I handed Skep Dollar the chrome 380 and I tucked the 9mm in my wristband, then he reached for the door ready to jump into action.

Dollar hold on, we got a change of plan.

What you mean, I know you am not getting scared on me now.

Naw hell Naw, I am not getting scared, it's just when you go in and start dumping shots, somebody got to watch out and when shit clear up, I can come in and help you with the money, we got to be safe on this one, lpok at the neighborhood we in.

He looked at me as if I had a point, but how will you know when shit is clear? You got your phone on you right?

Yeah I got it, he said.

We can stay on the call where I could hear everything and as soon as you ready you let me know and don't forget I seen him hide the money in the basement but I don't know exactly where but don't worry I know it's in there.

Alright, I got you but when I say that I'm ready, you better move fast Dollar said.

I will, and be carefully, one thing I know for sure is he has a lot of guns around the house so you have to shoot first and ask questions later, I said.

Don't worry he ain't got a chance in hell moving under this gun.

He jumped out the car, we locked eyes for a second and in that second, he had an unexplainable smile come across his face, one that can give you the chills, like you sitting in a movie theater, and the scariest part is about to happen. I watched Skep Dollar break into the dollar, I put the phone to my ear to hear what was going on inside the house, I could hear Skep Dollar immediately in the house raising hell asking about the money, while Money Mo and his woman beg for their life, then just like that, shots was fired, at that point I heard all I needed to hear, I ended the call, started the car and drove off leaving Skep Dollar behind, when I hit the comer I made a call to 911, reporting I seen a man break into a house, I gave them the address and that I heard shots fired so they need to hurry quick, then after I got off the phone with 911, I threw the phone out the window on my way to the express way.

Skep Dollar heard the phone hang up but only figured that maybe Lil Wright was on his way inside the house, he already shot Money Mo's bitch and would have shot him to but felt not just yet, he needed him to lead him to the money.

Man get the fuck off your knees and show me where this money at, for I do you just like I did that bitch Dollar said.

All right, I'll show you where the money is, just please don't kill me, said Money Mo.

Money Mo got off his knees, and moved next to the closet, he knew he had to at least make one attempt to save his life, he had been in the streets all his life and one thing he knew for sure is that when someone kills a motherfucker in front of you without a mask and you're the last witness, when they get what they want, you're going to be the last one to die, to keep a clean hand, all this is bad timing damn, my wife had been telling me to get out the game for years, tonight, we was celebrating me getting out, now she is dead and this is a situation I might not make it out of as well, but I got to try, Money Mo went into the closet and grabbed a duffle bag, concealing the 9mm he had hid with it, when he turned around he could see the look in Skep Dollars eyes, it showed a strong lust for greed.

Bring me that bag Motherfucker and hurry up, I got places I got to be, Dollar said.

Without willing to share another word Money Mo took one step and threw the bag in Skep Dollars direction, in the same motion, let off shots, boom, boom, boom, boom, boom, boom.

I'm going to kill your motherfucking ass, Money Mo said.

One of the shots hit Skep Dollar in the leg and another hit him in the stomach, forcing him back into the wall, as Dollar return fire pow, pow, pow, pow landing all shots, two went into his chest, one hit him in the throat, and the last one landing square inside Money Mo's face, the blood was pouring out of him uncontrollably and with each blink he can see Skep Dollar moving closer and closer to him, at this moment, all he could think about was his daughter and how his mother would know what to do, being that she had all his money, as Skep Dollar over him watching the smile cross his face, he raised his gun letting off two more shots into his head finishing the job, he should have finished from the jump, he wouldn't be shot if he would of just listened to Lil Wright, he went for the duffle bag to have a look inside, it was filled with newspapers and books with maybe ten thousand, touching the surface, he had been played and there was still no sign of Lil Wright, but he remembered, Lil Wright said he had the money in the basement, so he emptied the duffle bag, threw the money back inside the bag and headed for the basement, he could hear the sirens but he had to check, he didn't want all this to be for nothing and it would kill him if the police found the money and he didn't, when he got in the basement he searched everywhere, there was no money in sight, the sirens got closer and closer, I got to get out of here, he thought, disappointed from not finding much, he made his way to the door, only to see that he had been played for the second time tonight, Lil Wright had left him and there was nowhere for him to go, police cars started to surround the house and draw their guns.

Put the gun down and get the fuck on the ground, police screamed from behind their cars, ready to shot if Skep Dollar made any sustain movement.

Skep Dollar did what he was told, not knowing where life will take him next, police kept him at gun point, while the others rushed in to cuff and arrest him.

I had to move fast on getting to Money Mo stash before the calls started coming through about what happen to him. I pulled up to the house, it only took me like 15 minutes to get there, I hit the lights on the car and set for a while just to check out my surroundings, Money Mo had showed me this place one day when he was high and drunk out of his mind, speaking on how good life has been to him before he pulled two big garbage bags out the trunk and from its shape, you could tell that wasn't no clothes, I kept my eye on him the whole way, he went to the side of the house barely standing, I seen him go under a mat that was in front of the door and pull out a key, that's when I knew this was the spot, I got out the car and ran to the side of the house and checked the mat and the key was right where I suspected to be, I opened the door real slow, praying there isn't an alarm, it would not of stopped anything, I was just that hungry, it just would of made me move a whole lot faster, I wasn't sure the money was here but I had a real good feeling it is, I didn't hear an alarm sound off, so I knew everything was good, as I walked through the kitchen into the living room, I noticed the pictures on the wall was of Money Mo in his early childhood, and that's when it became clear to me that I am in Money Mo's momma spot, I moved slow up the stairs, I could see a bathroom light on, next to two rooms with both of the doors shut, at this point it became the luck of the draw, the first door I opened I could see an older woman, laying in her bed, having what it look like to be one of the sweetest dreams, that's about to turn into a nightmare real quick, I got close to the bed, reached out and placed my hand over her face covering her mouth and placing the gun to her head, leaning in close to speak my directions out in a whisper.

Is anybody else in this house? I asked.

My presents startled her out of her sleep, with fear in her eyes shook her head no.

Ok, now what I need you to do is be very quiet, get up and show me where the money is.

I moved my hand and she screamed, as loud as she could as soon as she got the chance, I hit her over the head as hard as I could, to shut her up, she rowed to the other side of the bed and fell on the floor, I snatched the phone out the wall, as I headed her way, her screams got louder, once I got close to her I stuck her two more times, just to let her know, this wasn't a game and that I mean business, she fell flat on her stomach, I put the gun to the back of her head and tied her hands behind her back.

What do you want? What do you want? I don't have nothing!

Don't play stupid with me bitch, if you don't give me what I want you gone die here tonight, I said.

Then you gone have to kill me cuz I ain't got shit for you!

Is that right huh, I grabbed her by the hair and forced her into the bathroom, throwing her face first into the tub, I put the tub plug in its place and turned the water on as hot as I can get it.

Now listen here lady, I am not come to show you no love, I'm telling you right now, you gone drown, if you don't give me the doe or the drugs.

She looked me right in my face and told me, Fuck you, you're a coward.

That's ok, you want it, you can get it, and I'll show you a coward, every second under the waters gone feel like an hour!

I grabbed her by the hair aggressively, forcing her face under water watching her feet kick as she struggles to breathe, I raised her head, seeing if she was ready to give me what I need, but her first words formed a question and that question was, why me?

I lost my patience and shot the gun right pass her face, pow, and that was the shot that put her in her place, she began to tell me where the money was,

It's in the basement, in an old gun safe, the key is hidden up in the fire place, I got all I needed to know from her, as I made a turn for the door, it flew open fast.

Grandma, I want, my, daddy.

Pow, pow, I shot off instantly, hitting the baby once in the chest and the other landed in her head, instantly killing her on impact, a sadness filled my heart but what I did I couldn't take it back, what was done was done, the grandmother went crazy, I was in a zone and that's the only thing that made me snap back into reality was her screams of pain.

You son of a bitch, you killed my baby, no, no, no, you killed my baby.

I raised the gun, its business over bullshit, then I shot her close range, in the head, her brains sprayed all over the wall, she fell face first and the faucet broke her fall. I ran down to the basement, I went straight to the fire place and that's where I found the key with no problem at all, when I opened the safe, I couldn't believe my eyes, there were five garbage bags full of money, just the sight, blew my mind, I started grabbing as much as I can, running to the car as fast as I can, I could hear sirens coming from a distance, I ran and got the rest of the money, jumped in the car and smoothly left the scene, I had one more stop to make before my mission could be complete, I headed to the storage unit, I knew once I stole that key it would come in handy, it was made like a two car garage, with one spot free so I pulled inside and shut the door so nobody would be able to see, I give it to Money Mo, he had a smooth plan, just made a couple fuck ups along the way, that I bet you, he would have never thought would of caught up with him one day. I went into Money Mo's old school 76 impala, in the trunk, there was another duffle bag of money and three bricks of cocaine, I hit my goal and more, I found the keys to the impala and put all the bags of money from Dollars car inside, then I wiped down the gun and the car making sure I left no evidence in or on the outside that can tie anything to me, I changed my clothes and put them in a bag but I took them with me, I wish I could of left my conscience in this garage as well but unfortunately that was another thing that I had to take with me, as I left the garage I closed a chapter in my life, I got all the money I could ever need, I framed Skep Dollar with the chrome 380, so he will be pinned down with Sunny murder along with the other two murders he just committed, and once they find Money Mo mom and daughter, that three murders is gone turn into five and with five bodies I could bet I will never have to worry about Skep Dollar ever again because he going to be spending the rest of his life in prison, the way I see it is its better him then me, fuck him, this was all a business move, if I would of told Skep Dollar where the money really was, he would not of spared my life, I would have been found dead in the house with the rest of them. As I ride behind the tent of the old school impala, I turned on some music because my thoughts were all over the place, I kept seeing visions of the baby I just killed, so I stopped at the light, looking for any CD

I could find in sight, I reached over to check the glove box and as I looked inside, I was startled by a knock on the window.

Money Mo, what's up bro, roll the window down so I could holla at you! Knock, knock, knock, Money Mo!

We both locked eyes for a second before I straighten up, grabbed the wheel and took off through the light, I was slipping and now I could only hope I didn't blow my position, I popped DMX into the deck, I noticed when I went into the glove box there was also a Glock 40 under the CD's, I pulled the Glock 40 out and put it on my lap and my eyes went to the rearview mirror as I drive listening to the music.

DMX: the snake, the rat, the cat, the dog, huh, how you gone see it, if you living in the flog The snake, the rat, the cat, the dog, ah huh, how you gone see it if you living in the flog.

I pulled up close to my grandma's house, even dough I knew I shouldn't have, I had to much shit to just be in the open walking around with, but I made sure I moved fast and I got everything in the house without anybody seeing me, now before the sun fully comes up, I got to get rid of this car.

Man ain't that Money Mo car, he said as he lay back in the car watching Lil homie get in the car and drive off, he remembered the Lil dude from when he would be riding around with Money Mo doing pickups.

Yeah that's his shit, he said to himself, Money Mo never let anyone drive his cars, he used to say that his cars were personal, he used to treat them like they were his babies, they were the only thing he felt he could truly keep to himself. Everything else he did or had was for his family. He knew that he should just mind his business, but something about the view of Lil homie just didn't feel right, so he pulled out his cell phone and tried to hit Money Mo line.

I at first thought, that I should torch the car but now I can't do that, all because of the guy that seen me at the light, so I decided to drop the car off next to one of Money Mo best friend's house, clean everything and leave the keys in the car, now when people start to see him drive, they won't think nothing of it, the way I see it, all the time people want to be seen, but I learned early that being seen will get you knocked off quick, so I know there was no way I was keeping the car, I'm the type who stayed in the shadows of my hustle, never letting the left hand know what the right one can do. On my way back to my grandma's house, I took the clothes I had on from last night and burned them in an alley far from where I dropped the car off, if I would have been thinking I would have grabbed the other clothes from my grandma's house, put them together and burned them all at the same damn time. That's what happens when you in the streets moving too fast, it could be a skip in a step that could destroy your life, May-so always said, you have to pay attention to detail. When I got to my grandma's house I went straight upstairs so I could count that money, it was so much money I didn't know what i was going to do or how I was going to hide it, as I was counting the money my grandma busted into the room her face showed a shit load of worry, she threw a garbage bag at me, stepped inside and shut the door behind her. When I looked inside, my heart just froze, I knew I had a lot of explaining to do and I didn't know where to start, she found the clothes from where I killed Sunny and caught me red handed counting the money. I told her about Sunny but I couldn't tell her everything, I blamed the murders from last night on Skep Dollar, I made it like he forced me and I took the money and left him out to dry but in my heart she knew the real, I couldn't let her see or know for sure the monster I had become and plus I didn't know what she would do with that information. I wondered could I really trust her, Trust is hard to come by where I'm from. What surprised me the most, she got close and kissed me on the forehead and said,

Baby what's done is done, but you can't tell nobody else about what happen and especially about this money, not even your momma, you hear me?

Yeah ma'am.

I mean it, no matter what!

We sat down and counted everything up and it came out to a little over 3 million, I swear it felt like forever how long it took to count the money, I went to sleep at least three times, almost losing count and I would have hated having to start over again. Between counting, me and my grandma made an agreement, that nothing will change, we both knew that people will be watching me, there was no guarantee that Skep Dollar would stay solid and not bring my name up especially once he found out that I set him up, instead of the two bodies he knew he was facing, turned out to be five, I had to be safe and just lay low, that's enough to make anybody roll over to the cops, I want to see if he hold up to the street code now, with his back this far against the wall.

Time has passed, I'm now 12 about to turn 13 years old, I did a little hustling but I made sure I slow paced everything, on a low level so I didn't bring any attention my way. I sold the whole 3 brinks I took from Money Mo, then I walked away from the dope game for a while. A part of me just wanted to see what the normal life felt like, you know, school, meeting new friends, girls, well yeah girls especially! I had one that was on my menu for sure, her name was Chrissy, she had a very contagious style, one that was hard to describe, she had one of the fattest asses and a cute set of tits that look like they stood at attention in an army line, I found out quick I was attracted to her lips because the fullness in hers always made my mind flip, I was addicted to this girl, to this world she is truly a gift. Them brown eyes kept me focused on her, I'm surprise she could fucking breathe, the only difference from me and her, she was 18, I lied to her and told her I was 16, it wasn't hard to believe because I definitely didn't act my age. She was a neighbor to one of my homeboys I met in school named Mike D, now that's my guy, real solid dude, he had my back on a situation where me and another dude got in a fight, after that we been best friends ever since. Truth be told Mike D had his eye on Chrissy to but I just bet him to the punch. Mike D has a Lil brother his name is Lil Will. Me and Mike D is the same age but Lil Will was 9 years old at the time, which is the same age I was when I started to move in the streets. Mike D would hate when his Lil brother would follow him around but not me, Lil Will always had this look in his eyes that spoke big things. He might have needed us now but who's to say that won't reverse. One day we were coming from the basketball court shooting some hoops, after we was done, we shot back to the house to grab something to eat, as always Mike D grandma's chicken was off the chain, before we walked into the house, I saw Chrissy stepping out of her house in the tightest shorts I have ever seen, they almost looked like they were painted on her body, a true master piece, she has a wide set of hips but somehow her pussy still managed to sit out in the front, I mean damn, if pussy could talk, hers would have a lot to say.

A Wright come here, let me holla at you.

I love when she would say my name, she always does something to me. I walked over to her and tried to quickly wrap her up in my arms.

Hi baby, I miss you, I said.

Uh Uh boy get off me, you always acting like my man when you come around, I haven't given you the pussy yet and you already acting crazy she said.

Ah uh the key word is yet! Doe baby doe I said.

She smiled and stepped to the side to make sure she can put on her serious face. Wright, what are you getting into this Sunday?

Not to mush for real baby just kicking it with the homies I said.

You and the homies can come over my house on Sunday, my momma is going to be gone to church all day, so we can chill and you know!

She moved closer and planted a wet passionate kiss on my lips, making my nature rise faster than an Olympian in a relay race, my heart started beating fast looking in her eyes, I got lost for words.

So what's up Wright, is you coming over? She said.

I snapped out of my thoughts, she placed me in, with a kiss Yeah, I'll be there, I said.

She looked down at my shorts as my dick poke through, putting a space between us, she looked both ways then took a step closer, spit in her hand then guided it down my shorts, stroking my dick up and down slowly while she was kissing my neck, unleashing her tongue on my ear, in circles. My eyes began to roll to the back of my head. She caught me in action, took a step back and began to laugh.

O I see I got you ready to pop already huh HA, HA, HA, she said.

No that just means that when you do give me that pussy, you in trouble. Ok, I guess, we will see baby, we will see she said.

I watched her walk away, looking back giving me the eye, the type of eye where you feel like a snack, I walked back over to Mike D'S house trying to catch me a plate before I went home for the night. His grandmother never minded me eating over there, she always talked about how respectful I was, so I always knew she looked at me as one of her own. When I came in, me and Mike D locked eyes, I knew he wanted to know everything that was going on and that's my boy, so of course I had to tell him what was going on. That's just what home boys do, put each other up on game. After we finished dinner, I said my good byes and headed towards the door, Mike D was on my heels.

Hold up, hold up, hold up bro you can't leave without telling me what happen, he said She wants us to come over Sunday, she said her momma going to be at church all day.

O yea, she must be trying to fuck!

Bro is she, she was in my shorts stroking my dick, licking all in my ear and shit, driving me crazy out that bitch, I said.

So what you going to do? Mike D said.

Fuck her, Ha, Ha, Ha, what you think I'm going to do I said.

Bro you ain't never fucked no bitch before, so don't even try to lie on your dick or bullshit me.

Naw, I haven't, but Sunday that's going to change for sure, plus when I was little I use to sneak and look at my uncle porno books, so I know a little something, shit I know more then you!

As Mike D just shook his head laughing at me, he stepped closer, his face became a little serious and his voice dropped down to a whisper.

A bro I got to holla at you about something, that kind of been on my mind for a while now. Talk to me, what's up what's good?

I been trying to figure out how I could put some money together, grandma been going through a real hard time with the bills and she ain't able to get the stuff me and Lil will need for school, so I got to do something. School is about to start again and we ain't got nothing put up for the new year, Mike D said.

I knew where this was leading, and I told myself I would stay clear of all the bullshit but this is my best friend, and I told him I would always have his back, so the least I could do is hear him out.

I'm listening, what you got in mind?

I know this chick like to run her mouth, always talking about how her step dad keep weed and that she knows where he hides it.

Who is this chick? Do I know her? I said Cassie,

Yeah, I know Cassie sexy ass, she hangs with big pussy Stacey Adams, I been trying to knock both of them down but they always acting stuck up,

Knock them down, what you mean?

I been trying to fuck both of them, did she tell you where the weed is hide at? I said.

No that's the point, we got to do our homework. Probably chill with them a Lil bit, you know they both like to smoke weed, so there is room to get in with them.

Michael, get in this house and get these dishes clean and that homework done so you can get ready for bed, Mike D grandma said.

Homework it's the summer, how you doing homework motherfucker?

You know I fucked up and I got to do this stupid ass summer school shit, but look I'm going to caught up with you later before she comes out here tripping and yeah we going to have to put something together, Mike D said.

We shook hands and parted ways. As I walked home my mind went into over drive. I wasn't hurting for any money, over the years my grandma Vickie been running all different types of investments, making sure my future is straight but on the other hand Mike D and Lil Will need me. I have never been the type to walk out on a friend, especially when they need me, but in the streets you got to look at situations from all sides. I know for sure Mike D isn't the type to rob anybody, so he has to be desperate, but most of all I have to be careful. A weakness is what it is, a weakness, so over these next couple of days I need to see what my next steps will be.

I walked into the house, checking for my mom, just to let her know I made it in the house safe. When we talk its always just a few words said, then I'm off, back to doing me, my mom has always been the type of woman who work hard, come home and give her man the rest of her time and attention. So we never had a bond but I understand, I think that comes from her never having a father in her life either. Word is, he got a lot of time in some other state and might not never come home. I always wondered about my father as well, I always wondered what he looks like or if he seen me on the street would he know who I am or would he walk right past me.

Every time I ask my mom about him, she would turn me down or believe me you don't want to know who he is, that answer has never been enough for me, so slowly I began my own search because I knew if I didn't find out who he is, a part of me would be just like my mom, empty inside with something missing. My momma's boyfriend was alright, besides the days he played super tough but I've learned how to hold my composure, you catch more bee's with honey, then running out naked with a net, that was something May-so told me and to tell you the truth, I still ain't got it all yet.

It's been a couple of days and I had a little time to think if I want to hit the move with Mike D or not and yeah it looks like I'm down, but it has to be worth it, there is nothing worse than doing something like this for nothing, you can lose your life for a mistake, so with that being said, I'm going to take my time and enjoy myself especially today, I'm not going to rush things, its Sunday, so I'm up early ready to go see Chrissy sexy ass, she been on my mind ever since our last Lil conversation. I got dressed and slid out the house without being noticed, I figured I slide to the store to get me some condoms, she might not have any and I don't need her trying to send me to the store while we thirty in the moment. As soon as I walked up to the door of the store, I seen Stacey Adams coming out with a baby stroller looking ratchet as hell, her hair wasn't done, nails weren't done, in some dirty socks and flip flops, but she thick as hell doe in some tight pajama pants, when she walks her ass cheeks clap with every step, Stacey also got these real big lips that come with an over bit, but believe me, I'll go, shit I'm just another horn ball, trying to chase a nut.

What's up Stacey, I see you looking really good today.

Boy why you lying I came outside looking a hot mess, I just had to grab a couple of things from the store, and why you talking to me anyway? Any other time you see me, you don't have no words for me, Stacey said.

Damn, I can't feel good today, acknowledge your booty, I mean your beauty at its finest.

Boy whatever, what's good doe? When you going to come through and chill, maybe smoke with me?

We can set that up, is you going to hook me up with your girl Cassie? I been crushing on her for a while now. I said.

What, since when? And you mean you been giving me all them eyes like you like me, but you really want to fuck with my girl!

I mean both of you'll is sexy as hell!

O so you trying to smash me and the homie?

She walked around me in circles, showing me every inch of her body and I ain't going to lie, I might have to try her later but for now I have to keep everything all business.

Stacey come on now, is you gone pass her the word for me? Yeah I guess!

And yeah my boy Mike D been feeling you for real too, maybe we can all hook up and do a double date or something and don't worry, tell her it's all on me.

O is that right, so you balling now huh? You know you ain't fucking with no cheap bitches, you ain't about to treat us to no Wendy's meal, Stacey said.

When I heard what she said I had to laugh even dough her face told me that she was dead ass serious.

No baby where ever you'll want to go, just hit me up and let me know and we there.

I wrote down the number and stood for a while just to watch Stacey walk away, and she knew I was looking and I was glad she did, you get more out of women when your emotions aren't hidden, I planted the seed, but I'm not going to bring it to Mike D just yet, first she needs to call, we make the connection then we can go from there. After I get what I need from the store I headed straight to Chrissy house. When I knocked on the door, Chrissy answered in a nice Lil tight fitted dress, with her legs shining like she poured on a whole bottle of baby oil, smelling like something tropical from bath and body works, as I looked behind her I could see Mike D and Lil Will was already in the spot, so I came right in and parked a sit on the couch.

Damn baby, you rude, you just going to come in and don't give me a kiss, or a hug or nothing, Chrissy said.

Baby you gone get something started if I touch you So what's wrong with that?

She smiled as she walked away to the kitchen, when she got in the door way she pulled her dress up a little just to show me she didn't have any panties on.

Baby grab a blunt off the table and come back here with me for a minute, Chrissy said.

Mike D looked at me and smiled, then shook his head, I did as I was told, but in very slow steps, I was nervous. My heart began to pound the closer I got to the back room, then out of nowhere she pulled me into the bathroom, and began to kiss me slowly and passionately on my lips, then my neck, then my chest, then she stopped.

Baby light that blunt up and relax.

I had never smoked a day in my life until now, until I was with Chrissy, with each puff I could feel the smoke enter my lungs and a tingle ran all over my body, and damn when she touched me it drove me crazy. She unbuttoned my pants then got on her knees and took me slowly into her mouth keeping her eyes set on me the whole time, deep throating my dick, over and over I watched all of me disappear, to doing tricks on the tip, she took complete control and I gave it to her, then she stood up and took the blunt from out of my hands.

Come on baby, it's your turn now, I want you to taste me.

She moved to the toilet, dropped the lid then sat on top and spread her legs wide open. I got on my knees and began to kiss her pussy with soft kisses, I never did this before so I didn't know what to do, I followed her lead keeping eye contact.

Come on baby lick this pussy, suck this pussy for momma make me cum all in your mouth.

I began to take long licks, like her pussy was an ice cream cone, I didn't leave her ass out I treated them both the same, she began to go crazy, holding the back of my head tight, pushing my face in and out her pussy, I could taste her sweet juices, the more I sucked and worked my tongue, she opened up her clique for me and it became an victim, I learned the faster I go the more she couldn't control herself, my dick was throbbing, I couldn't take it no more I had to feel myself inside her, so I got off my knees, then pulled out the condom, she took it from me because I guess I was taking too long and got back on her knees licking and sucking all over my balls, making my dick extra hard, then in one motion she put the condom in her mouth and rolled it onto my dick, deep throating me, slobbing all over me, I took the back of her head and began to pound my dick into her throat, she backed up and laid completely on her back opening her legs wide, I knew just which place to go because my tongue had just visited her sweet spot, when I entered inside her I could feel her walls gripping me, fighting me as I open her up with every stroke, her pussy began to build pressure, I backed out as if something was wrong. Her juices flew all over my chest and stomach, she began to reach for me to come back inside of her, so I could give her more, I pounded her tight wet pussy harder and harder and then suddenly there was a knock at the door.

No baby please don't stop, baby don't stop, you ain't got to answer the door come on give me some more, Chrissy said.

I stood up and opened the door to see who was on the other side, Mike D was standing there touching himself, as he passed me the blunt, I pulled him inside the bathroom, I began to smoke the blunt making space letting him move into my place, as he was putting the condom on, Chrissy sat up and began to rub his dick all over her face, as she put him into her mouth, she got him rock hard, then she turned her pretty ass around and stuck it all the way up in the air, looking back at Mike D to invite him inside, he got down on his knees behind her spread her cheeks entered her and began to pound her as hard and as fast as he can. She watched me the whole time, licking her lips, showing me that she was enjoying his every stroke that he unleashed inside of her. Within minutes I noticed how Mike D started to get weak inside of her, as she pushed and bounced her pussy up and down his dick, he moaned as she moaned, I got turned on watching every second, and then he came. Without missing a beat Mike D stood up walking like he had lost feeling in his thighs, he went out the door, not even stopping to look back, I locked it. I turned around, the only thing on my mind was getting more of her. I took the condom off, damn I had to feel her walls bear skin, shit I might be crazy for doing this but I have too, and with her I'm willing to take the chance, I enter inside her and started back stroking her wet walls, feeling every bit of her, damn her pussy tightly wrapping around me, talking to me, on its own, not in the English language, I could feel the power she was taking from me. I had to switch positions just to last a little longer, when she began to ride me, I got lost in her eyes, I could feel my feet curl and I could feel myself ready to release between her thighs, damn baby I'm Cumming, she jumped up real fast placing me in her mouth sucking hard, and but slow, finishing the job, as I bust all in her mouth and all over her face. In that moment, I just knew I had fell in love with her, not by heart, but by her nasty ways, today we shared something real special that I know neither one of us will ever forget, as she jumped into the shower, I washed my body off in the sink, leaving her to take care of her business as I go make me a plate, I just wanted to eat and smoke then eat again, plus do my best to relax from the love making we just made. What blows my mind is me and Mike D just lost our virginity to the same woman on the same day.

After I left Chrissy's house, I got home kind of late, I got me a shower, letting all the thoughts of what happen today flow through my head, damn I could still feel her touching me and I have a strong craving for the taste of her, that I wonder, if the next woman could ever replace her. I got in the bed getting ready to call it a night, then the phone rang.

Hello,

What's up Lamar What's up who is this.

I knew it had to be family, because nobody else would just call me by my first name.

This your aunt Sharon boy, your uncle Scottie wife, I wanted to know if you wanted to go with me to visit him tomorrow?

Hold up now, is this your way of asking me out on a date? Because if so, you don't have to shoot me no codes and I know how to keep a secret, I said.

Boy stop playing, I just wanted to know if you wanted to ride with me!

Naw Sharon is a real live cutie, if she gave me a chance, I would fuck her, I would be a fool not too. She has two kids but her body is off the chain, she is very smart and just a real live sweetheart, all the way down to the core. I really love being around her, it almost feels like I'm breaking her in more and more. If my uncle breaks her heart, I'm gone be all over him, then shit, I might have a chance with her.

I don't know, I might be a Lil busy tomorrow.

Don't act like that Lamar, I want you with me, and lunch will be on me after, Sharon said Alright I'll go, just hit me up in the morning.

Ok, you just make sure you ready, don't have me come down there for nothing Lamar. Ok, I love you baby.

Ah huh, and then she laughed before hanging up the phone.

I guess it will be nice to go see my uncle Scottie, especially since I haven't seen him in a while, he been down on a rape case, the judge gave him 4 years, it was just one of them fucked up situations, where he didn't want to be with the chick, so she did whatever she could do to hurt him, I guess someone taught her killing a good man name is enough pain for anybody to bear. Plus, while I'm there I could ask a couple of questions about my dad, my uncle and him was good friends for a long time, back in the day so I know he should be able to give me some type of information about the man at least I hope he can.

When I woke up the next morning, I still wasn't feeling the trip to see my uncle, mainly because it's hard to see someone you love locked down, caged up like a dog, but no matter what, you have to show them you love them, I know it could get tough up there alone. After I got up and got dressed my sexy aunt Sharon was outside blowing the horn, waiting for me, it took me a minute to come out, I was trying to finish the blunt I was smoking and at the same damn time hide the smell, which was crazy all in itself, even dough aunt Sharon is cool, she still had her days where she would act like the fuckin police. When I jumped in the car, o my God she smelled so damn good, I loved her sent, her perfume filled up the whole car, shit if I would of knew that shit it would not have taken me twenty more minutes to get ready, today she looked like steak, ready to be eaten, she had on a sun dress that hugged her body just right and she has these damn tits that sit up like she fresh out of high school, I could see her nipples poking through. She turns me on every time I'm around her, anytime a woman put those damn dresses on I always wonder if they got anything on under them. I got in the car looking fly dressed to impress just to see if I can catch her eye, from time to time she be making her Lil comments, like, if only you were a little older or you would be my Lil boyfriend if I wasn't with your uncle and if he keeps playing I'm going to put you on the team. She just doesn't know I take all them words to the heart, and plus I think it's a lot of truth to her words, but she always acting like she just joking.

Damn boy, what took you so long? You had me waiting forever, you going to make us miss the damn visit.

You know I had to look good for my baby, I said.

O here you go, you just don't stop, you gone make me tell your uncle on your ass, and you look high as hell, have you been smoking?

What makes you think you was the one I was trying to look good for is you my baby? And naw, I am not high, you tripping, I just woke up.

Naw, your ass ain't just woke up, you high as fuck!

I just laughed and laid the seat back, seeing if I can get into the music and enjoy the ride, and maybe if it's possible, my high, she threw on her angry face, turned the radio off and pushed me as hard as she could.

When the hell you start smoking Lamar?

At that point I couldn't hold back any longer, the words just rolled off my tongue before I could get the chance to get in control of it.

Around the same time, I started eating pussy!

I could tell I caught her off guard, her face had the evidence all over it O so now you having sex and doing drugs, O so you grown now?

I'm grown enough to know how to play the right position.

And what's that supposed to mean? Sharon said as she continued with her evil eye. That I'm good on keeping secrets and placing bets.

Secrets, like what secrets Lamar?

Secrets between us and bets, like if you just give me one chance you wouldn't regret it.

After I said what I said, a strong silence filled the car for the rest of the ride. I couldn't tell if she was mad at me or actually thinking about what I said. I could tell, the wheels in her brain was turning doe. We pulled up to the prison getting ready to go in but one of the guards had informed us we won't be able to visit because somebody ended up getting stabbed. But he said that we can catch my uncle on his outside rec if we hurry up, so we rushed around the comer to try and get a couple of minutes in with him. When I got around the corner, I spotted my uncle Scottie chilling with some guy, who was looking at me like we knew each other, I called over to my uncle, he started walking towards me and the guy followed smiling hard in my direction, all I could think is, now here go one of them cheesy ass conversations about how I grew up and you ain't seen me since I was a kid, I was not in the mood for that shit at all.

What's up uncle Scottie, it's good to see you, old man.

So this is Mr. Lamar Wright huh? The man said speaking over my uncle, rudely forcing his self into our conversation.

What's up man, do I know you? I asked.

Well you don't know me but you should, the man said.

And why do you think I should know you, you don't look important! Lamar! Sharon said.

It's ok, the man said.

Sharon walked up and held my hand like she was about to announce that we now are a couple, then she turned to me with a very soft tone and said, baby this is your dad, the words played a melody in my head but could not catch a tune.

He's my dad!

Yeah I wanted to surprise you at the visit, I heard you been searching for him and I just wanted to help. Sharon said.

I became lost for words, I didn't know what to say or how to say it, I just stared into the eyes of the man I been looking to meet for years.

Hey son, I also didn't want her to tell you, I really wanted to tell you myself face to face, so don't be mad at Sharon it's really not her fault.

I held Sharon's hand tight and tried to lean in for a kiss. I ain't mad at my baby,

As Sharon jumped back with the act of shock, she looked for my uncle to put in a word, I moved towards the man that claim to be my dad, I had so many questions, but from the moving of the guards, not enough time, only a couple of words was shared between us.

So what's up son, you into getting to know your dad?

Yeah that's cool, just hit me up sometime, we can catch up.

Then just like that I watched him walk away with all my unanswered questions and I could only wonder would he really call or would I bump into him 13 more years from now, this time maybe at a grocery store, at least this time I would know who he is if he walked by, when I got back into the car my mind was all over the place, I needed to slow my thoughts down, so I began to start rolling up a blunt.

Lamar, what the fuck is you doing? Sharon said.

I quickly snapped back into reality, I had forgot not only who I was with, but also where I was at. I'm rolling up this blunt, shit, I got a lot on my mind, this shit is crazy.

What's so crazy about it, you kept saying how you wanted to meet your dad, so now you did. I also keep saying I want some of that pussy, but you ain't trying to give me none of that.

Disrespect me one more time and I'm going to punch you in yo shit Lamar, and I'm serious think I'm playing!

Ok, ok, I'm sorry, I'm gone hit my breaks, I ain't going to sweat you no more and that's a promise.

Don't make this about me, just tell me how you really feel about the situation. To tell you the truth, I don't know how to feel.

I laid back and lit the blunt.

And make sure you pass that shit this way, she said.

Only way I'm passing this blunt is if we bonded in blood, I don't need you smoking with me and then telling on me later.

Boy from what I see, you gone do what you want to anyway, 12 going on 22 running around smoking blunts and eating pussy, shit crazy!

I passed the blunt laid back and didn't say another word, 10 minutes into the ride back home my phone rang.

Hello, who is this, I asked Who you want it to be?

In my mind, I had no clue, who it could be, I just got this phone, plus I couldn't recognize the voice at all.

I just know by this sexy Lil voice, it's got to be someone special, a special little gift wrapped just for me.

Ha, ha, ha, something like that, this is Cassie, Stacey gave me the number and told me that you wanted me to get at you, so I thought I'd call and say hello.

Yeah I been thinking about you like crazy, wondering when you were going to call me.

Right after I said them words, I looked over at Sharon, I could see her cutting her eye at me, almost showing signs of jealousy, trying to tune into my conversation, wondering who I'm talking too, the thought just made me laugh, I continued with my conversation.

I want to hook up with you, if you let me, I want to take you on a date.

Yeah, Stacey told me what was up, and that's cool, if you for real, then we could make that happen.

If I'm for real, yeah I'm for real, what you gone wear?

Boy, lol, why you worried about what I'm gone wear, just know it's gone be nice and you gone like it.

I bet I am, so could we all hook up on Friday, I said Yeah, we can do that, Friday it is.

Ok cool baby, I'm gone lock your number in my phone and make sure I see you on Friday. Ok, see you later, bye.

We hung up the phone, and all I could think about is not just how sexy she is but also how close.

I am to the next move, I talked Sharon into dropping me off at Mike D's spot, I had to feel him in on what's going on with the date, with Cassie and Stacey.

Mike D what's up brother?

Shit, just chilling high as fuck, ready to get up and make me something to eat.

Well before you get up and start feeding your face, I got some good news to lay on ya.

O yeah, what good news you got for me, shit I hope it's about some money, while I'm sitting over here with these fucked up pockets.

Well something like that, I got us a double date with Cassie and Stacey, I said.

Cut the bullshit, how in the hell did you manage to pull that off? And which one I got?

Mike D looked like a kid in the candy store as soon as he heard the news, I couldn't tell if it was about the money or the pussy.

You got Stacey, I got Cassie fine ass, I caught Stacey at the store and told her I was feeling Cassie, I shot Stacey the number to give to her and she just called me today so it's on.

Naw mafucka, how did you pull that shit off? It's got to be more to it. Mike D said.

I told them that I would pay for ever thing when we take them out on our date.

Man see, I knew it was a catch to it, and how we gone do that? Our broke ass ain't got no damn money so what we going to do now? I can't be going nowhere broke looking like a lame, why you ain't talk to me first before you go making them,

Mike D chill bro damn, I got us, I got some money put up, where we can all go out and have a great time, plus this gives us the chance to get the real info on the step Dad.

Mike D got up and began to pace the floor as if what I just said completely took over his thoughts.

Hell yeah, we need to hit that lick, I heard that, that mafucka holding on to a lot of cash, he said.

Yeah but you can't listen to what everybody says, that's why we got to see what's going on for our self. Now when we get with the girls don't make it obvious we trying to get information out of them, just lay back and be cool, I said.

I got this bro don't trip, plus I been wanting to fuck the shit out of Stacey thick ass! Lol I hope you don't fuck her like you did Chrissy, minute man, I said.

Man fuck you bro, that was my first time plus that shit was wet as fuck!

We both laughed about what happen on that day, we smoked a couple more blunts and then I left on my way home. Today was a crazy day with me meeting my dad. Somehow I pictured things to be different but life is like that, you just don't know what to aspect from life. When I got to the house, my mom was sitting on the couch, eating her dinner, watching TV, I couldn't hold back what I found out, I had to tell her, the main reason is I had to see her reaction.

What's going on momma? How was your day?

Boy I'm tired, they worked me like a slave today, I couldn't wait to get off work so I can just watch my Lil TV shows and relax, until I do it all over again tomorrow, but enough about me how was your day, what you get into today, she asked.

Well, I went with Sharon to go see uncle Scottie.

How is your uncle doing? I been meaning to go up there and see him but I just been too damn busy with this job, mom said.

Yeah he doing ok, while I was up there I met my dad for the first time, as well. Hold up boy you did what?

As anger covered her face, I guarded myself from what look to be an unleash of punches coming my way.

Sharon took me to meet my dad, I said.

And why would the fuck she take you to do something as stupid and worthless as that? She said.

Because I been searching for him for a while now momma, so all she wanted to do is help out, and every time I ask you about him, you always say the same thing, (believe me you don't want to know him) I said.

O baby, believe me you don't, that man ain't for the right and he don't give a shit about you, when you get the chance ask him where he been all these years and why he ain't been in your life before now.

He probably gone say because of you, which is probably true since you hate him so much.

Lol is that what you think? That I kept him from you all these years. The only thing I ever tried to keep you was safe. But you growing up and you got to learn a lot of lessons on your own. All I ask is don't give him my number and don't show him where we live, you hear me?

Yes, ma'am.

I watched my mom in the conversation about my dad have 3 to 4 different faces of emotion, but the last one ended in deep compassion mixed with a strong worry, and I think it was that moment that made me wonder was all of this coming from a place of hate for my dad or was he just that damn bad, it gave me doubt in him, I knew what to aspect from my mother, it was him I didn't know about, but the want to have something or someone can beat out common sense in a race any day. That was what May-so would tell me all the time when I was on my way to do something stupid I might regret later, but I have to go with this, I have to find out on my own, if I don't I would just wonder for the rest of my life. Damn curiosity will get you killed, it's even worse with the heart, I went back outside, I needed to clear my mind, I looked at my phone and noticed I missed a couple calls from Stacey, I hit redial to call her back, it didn't take no time for her to answer the phone.

Hello,

What's up Lamar, what you doing?

Shit I'm just chilling, trying to clear my head.

What's up, what's wrong baby, can I help you clear your mind? She said Lol, now how you gone help me clear my mind!

Boy don't go there, you can come over and we can smoke and talk, I'm here for you if you need a shoulder to lean on, I ain't say nothing about some pussy.

I didn't either, I just asked you how would you clear my mind, then you spoke on the pussy, but I ain't gone lie a little would be nice.

Man whatever, is you coming over to chill or not Lamar? I'm trying to smoke, I ain't smoked all day, I know you got some weed and I got a Lil bottle, what's up? She said searching for my answer.

So is Cassie coming through or should I call Mike D and tell him to meet over there?

Naw, it's just going to be me and you, you act like we can't be alone, what's wrong with that, you act like two friends just can't chill without getting out of pocket!

I didn't say nothing was wrong with it, I just asked a question damn chill Stacey.

By Stacey continuing to get defensive, I could tell she wanted more, then she leads on, and I have the choice to bit or not.

Ok Stacey just chill alright, I'll be over there in a minute, just be looking out for me. Ok hurry up doe!

We hung up, and I headed to her house, when I got there, I could tell I was on the right track in my thoughts. When she answered the door, damn, she was a complete different person I seen at the store, plus it was almost as if she didn't have nothing on, she was wearing a something that looked like a muscular shirt that looks like it was made into a dress, she was oiled up from head to toe, her hair was done, hands and feet were matching, baby really had her shit together today, my mind started flipping, I started to question why did I come here in the first place, I don't want to fuck shit up with Cassie, to my surprise we talked, and smoked a couple blunts, a Lil liqueur was passed around, we talked some more, she cooked and we ate, over the course of time I could tell things was starting to loosen up, I learned that me and Stacey really has a lot in common, we got more like then dislikes in this world and it really made me look at her differently. One thing I noticed over time, is she began to touch me more and more, or she would place her legs over mine, and from time to time she would expose a Lil bit to me at a time. Plus, she smelled good as fuck, I was really to make a move I didn't know if that was the right thing to do but she was turning me on the longer we were in each other's company, my mind was telling me that I should just get up and get out of there but no part of my body is even to make an attempt to move to the door, I could see her eyes, searching for any weakness inside of me, by the minute I was losing, let's just say if this is a test, then I'm failing badly. She has my fttii attention, before I knew it my dick was rock hard, poking through my jeans, to the point I couldn't hide it from her sight, I lost control and my desire to want her grew more and more by each minute, so I broke the oddness between us and made a move on her.

Lamar, what is you doing?

At this point I don't know, I got so much on my mind and by the way you handling me in here you got me thinking you feeling me.

Yeah I am feeling you, but you made your choice and this ain't right, Cassie my girl, and you already said you feeling her, I can't just fuck you.

Ok, then let me taste you!

The look on her face told me she wanted me to do just as I spoke so I got on my knees and crawled between her legs to see would she stop me along the way, to my surprise she opened up to let me in, I started kissing the soft spots of her thighs, then she put up a small fight, pushing my head away but was over powered by the feeling of wanting more, it took time but she slowly started to received me as I turn her on in all the right places, once I got her legs to open up as wide as I could get them to go, I took in the view of her pussy and admiring just how beautiful it truly was, her clique stood out demanding attention and attention was what I gave her as I open her up with both hands so I could see clear what was hiding inside, I took her clique into my mouth and began to suck on it as hard as I could, learning the difference from what she wanted to what she needed, taking long licks up and down, round and round until I could taste her thick sweet juices cum all in my mouth, my performance was based off the rise in her voice or the arc in her back, and I loved when she called my name though I got scared we would get busted from how loud we got I just couldn't stop, I enjoyed every minute I shared with her, we made a mess, she dripped all the way to her ass, which I didn't hesitate to clean up, I flipped her over in a doggy style position, I wanted her bad, I had to be inside of her, I wanted to be the one to break all her walls down. Shit, I had already gone this far, why not go a little bit farer, why not finish what I already started, I forced my pants down around my ankles as fast as I can, as I rub my dick up and down the crease of her pussy, teasing her hole, I moved forward to slide inside, she jumped up moving my dick out the way.

I told you, I can't fuck you Lamar!

Damn we already went this far we might as well keep going, I said.

We both know you want to be with my friend and that ain't right we can't do this.

At that moment, I was willing to say anything just so we could finish what we had going on, just so this shit wouldn't end. But at the same time I had to be smart, even in a moment like this, I had to cut my Lost's, it wasn't worth losing out on Cassie or fucking up the move all together.

You right, I'm sorry, I don't know what got into me.

I reached for my pants, with a strong disappointment covering my face.

It's alright, we just got to feeling the drank and we smoked all them blunts, getting high, so shit could happen, so shit look, don't trip I ain't gone say nothing, this gone be just between you and me, this is our Lil secret.

Then she stepped in slowly and delivered a kiss on my lips, to sucking her juices off of them. As I got the rest of my things and headed for the door, Stacey stopped me in my tracks.

Lamar, where you going, you can't leave yet.

I figured you wanted me to leave after everything that just happened.

Yeah I can see how you would think that, but it's only fair if I return the favor you gave me, then it would truly be a secret between us.

She moved me to the couch, taking my pants off completely, making sure I'm as relaxed as I could get before she got between my legs and filled her mouth with as much of me as she could fit. I watched as she slowly bobbed up and down eyes closed moving to her own rhythm as if she was in tune with her favorite song, my mind was free, wondering out in to space, damn was this what making love truly felt like, finding yourself inside another and loving every minute of it, my time was up out of nowhere, I exploded all in her mouth and with what was left, she played with on the tip of her tongue, holding me tight rubbing me all over her lips, with her eyes open, she cleared every thought I had, I just laid there stuck in one place not able to move, damn she was a beast.

Shit you ok Lamar?

Yeah baby I'm straight, trying to act as if what she just done to me was nothing. I had to sound tough, but in truth, she really just blew my mind, I knew that if she let me, I would probably move in, I had a feeling, things were not done with us, her place was going to be a revolving door for me, I just became a fiend for her touch.

Did you like it?

Yeah it was cool, look we got to do this again some time, as I stood up to put my pants back on. She looked at me like I offended her by my words.

It was just cool huh, well it seemed like it was more than that, the way your toes were curling.

Me and Stacey laughed and talked for a little while longer before I left. It had been a while since I saw May-so, so I had to go touch bases with him to see what's been going on in the streets.

May-so always kept his ears to the street, his favorite line is, I do the work so you won't have too, I make the mistakes so you never will, and one thing I could always say about May-so is he has always had my back anytime I needed him. When I got to May-so house, everything was all but normal, the man was high out of his mind, naked, with dope laying around everywhere.

May-so what's going down, tell me something good, I said.

Ain't nothing going on young blood, it's just the same old shit, going on around here, dope and dollars, dollars and dope. What's going on with you?

I told May-so about me meeting my dad for the first time and how he talked about getting to know me, I vented to him about how my momma acted and about all the things she had to say about him, the whole time May-so didn't say a word, all he did was listen, waiting patiently until my conversation came to a stop and when it did, he didn't hesitate to share his thoughts.

I know you are excited about meeting your dad and that's a good thing, but it also could be some truth to what your mom is telling you as well so guard your heart young blood, I ain't saying that you shouldn't get to know him, I'm just saying be careful.

Be careful why? This is my Dad; why would he want to hurt me?

It's not about him hurting you, it's about you living outside your emotions, don't never let a man get a hold of your bottle and baby sit your cup at the same time. May-so said not making any sense to me.

What? What the fuck is that supposed to mean?

Man up and listen to me, when a man rides behind you in the back sit of your car, he's got a hold of your bottle, your bottle is the control of the situation, which is your life. If somebody else is pouring ain't no telling how much you will drink!

Ok, May-so I could see you high right now I'll come back later.

Boy, listen to me, you control the bottle you control your situation, you control your cup, you control your life which mean, never give someone your gun, no matter who it is and especially if they sitting behind you, that's like just giving your life away, Lamar do you got a Lil dope on you.

I told him no to the dope but I held on to his words, even dough I know he was high as a kite, his words were sharp as a knife, cutting into my very soul, everything was always deep with May-so even dough it might seem complex with May-so, the message is very simple, watch who you trust with your life, afler all, you only got one, after I left May-so, I was once again built up with a whole bunch of thoughts, it makes me think about going back to Stacey house to see if I could clear everything up again, Lol, a second round, on second thought, I'll just call it a day.

Over the last couple of days, I kept in touch with Cassie and Stacey, as far as me and Stacey talking, it's starting to look like a Lil creep thing between us, she might even be catching some Lil feelings for me, today is the day that we all are going on our double date. I just hope none of what me and Stacey did, comes out or blows up in my face. I haven't told Mike-D about me and Stacey either, that shit is to good, I have to keep that my Lil secret, plus I don't think this is a good time to tell him, because it would only throw things off if he gets in his feelings about us. We might have lost our virginity together but other than that I don't think he is the sharing the woman type. We all went to a nice little restaurant called Longhorn, we all ate, laughed, and had a good old time. Me and Stacey didn't skip a beat, you would have never thought we been moving on the low, but I would catch her every once in a while giving me the eye, a lot of the time Mike D acted real timid, so I figured I turn things up a notch.

Hey so what's up y'all, how about we go grab a bottle and go roll up at the park, I said What park? Stacey said.

It's one over in Newport Kentucky that's right next to the river, and it's out the way, so ain't no police gone pop up on us or nothing, it could be fun, I said.

Cassie stared off as if she was interested in the conversation at all.

What's wrong baby? I asked as I wrapped my arms around her.

I don't know, I told my mom I wouldn't come in the house hate and I can't afford to get in trouble, shit I just got off punishment. Cassie said.

Girl, you gone be alright, we ain't gone be over there long, damn stop acting like a prude! Stacey said.

Girl fuck you! said Cassie.

I grabbed Cassie up by her waist, pulling her body in close to mines, making sure our eyes reached an eye to eye contact level.

Baby could you stay just a Lil bit longer for me, I want to

spend a little more time with you, I don't want to let the night end so early. I said.

How long is you talking about? Giving me the eye as if she ain't playing when it comes to the answer.

Not long baby, I'll make sure you at the house at a nice hour, I promise.

It took Cassie a minute to agree but once she did, we were on our way to the park. When we got there I made sure we put some distance between Stacey and Mike D, I just wanted us to be alone so we could do our own thing. The more I talk to Cassie, the more I realize just how good and sweet of a person she truly is, and over time I could tell that I was falling for her, we talked about any and everything, I could just tell she was different. She really listened to me, I'm sure it's things she knew about me my own momma doesn't know and that rare for me because I have always been a private person, but she made it easy to open up to her in ways I couldn't imagine. I know we are young but I have actually thought about creating a family with her and could only wonder if she feels the same way about me. In at least 10 times tonight I kissed her, we held hands for long periods of time, I was catching feeling for her quick, I could see the mood was set just right for something special to happen, while I held her from behind I began to grind into her, I wanted her to feel my dick rise in between her ass cheeks, she had on a mini squirt, so this is the perfect time to try to slide inside her.

Baby what is you doing? She said Nothing baby why you say that?

Cuz it looks like to me, you trying to get in my pants, she said What's wrong with that?

A lot is wrong with that, when we make love for the first time I want it to be special and ain't nothing special about laying on your back in the park.

You said the first time, does that mean with me or your first time ever, I said.

It's my first time ever, I have never been with anybody else, I'm not like Stacey, I mean, she is my best friend and I love her but she is a little, you know Cassie said with a look not wanting to speak the words herself.

What? A little loose.

Yeah, and I am not like that at all. Cassie said.

Meanwhile, while we were talking, we notice that Mike D and Stacey had disappeared, so this was a good time to get a little more personal.

Baby I want to be 100% honest with you, I don't want to leave anything out, when it comes to me.

Ok, what is it baby, you could tell me anything!

I been hustling in the streets for a while now and I'm really good at it, I just been having a problem finding the right people to take me to the next level, baby with the right connect, I could make enough money to move away, get a head start for when I start my family one day.

Cassie's eyes lit up with joy once she heard those words.

Lamar, money don't make you happy, my mom and step dad have plenty of money and they still argue and fight all the time.

Yeah but your mom and step dad don't have a love like ours, I love you and if you let me, one day I hope I could marry you.

As soon as I said those words, I could tell that I had melted her heart. She was feeling me, I knew she was, I could see it in her eyes.

You love me?

Yeah baby I do, did I say something wrong? I asked No, you didn't say anything wrong.

She looked me in the eyes as tears began to form in her face. She held me as tight as she could as we both stared out into the river, everything about this moment just fGlt special I truly enjoyed her company and to tell the truth, a part of me didn't ever want this to end. I kind of felt bad a little bit because I knew things wasn't going to end well, unless I could hit the move on her dad without her finding out it was me. That way me and Cassie could still be together, things just have to be done right. We left, I made sure she made it home at a respectable hour, then I headed home to call it a night myself.

When I woke up the next morning, I noticed I missed a couple calls from an unknown number. I figured that if it was important then they would call me back, today I just wanted to relax and enjoy my day the best way that I could, so I figured I slide down to Washington Park and shoot some hoops with Mike D when I got down to the court Mike D was shooting hoops with this guy named Lil Rob, I didn't like Lil Rob to much because to me, he was nothing but a follower, man I hate a person who can't stand up on they own two feet, they always following behind the next man. The type of guy that hides behind somebody else identity and for that reason I have no respect for him at all, but I know how to play it cool, just with them type of guys you got to be careful, because they could be the type to knock you down in the long run.

What's up with y'all can I get a game in? I said.

Yeah if you ready to get your ass beat, you can Lil Rob said showing confidence in his eyes.

Cut the shit, you know you can't stop me on this court. But any way, what's been going on with you Lil Rob? I thought you had some Lil chicks lined up for us, at least that's what you said the last time we talked, I said.

O yeah Lil Rob! Damn you ain't invite me to this Lil party, Mike D said.

Naw hold up, I do have something nice for us, if you gone come over to my spot tonight. My mom and dad gone be gone so the spot gone be popping, Lil Rob said.

And what the fuck is that supposed to mean? I asked.

We gone have a Lil party tonight, that's what the fuck I mean!

See now that's what I'm talking about a little action, I said Yeah I told you I'll come through for us.

Cool, we might as well hang out until later tonight.

Bro I don't even have nothing to wear, I'm gone need some time to get ready Mike D said Listen none of y'all trip, we about to go hit the mall, it's all on me, I said.

You been saying that a lot lately Mike D said What!

It's on you, you been coming up on a lot of money and treating everybody and shit, you ain't cutting your boy in, what's up what's good, put me in the game coach, Mike D said.

I laughed it off but at the same time I noticed Mike D is starting to watch my moves more and more so I better slow things down a lot.

Bro I been stacking my money up to the ceiling, you know I been cutting grass all summer with my big cousin, I said.

Since when, nigga you always with me most of the time, when the hell you got time to cut some mafuckin grass, yeah right cut the shit, Mike D said.

Man you don't know what I be doing in my spare time, I don't be with you all the damn time either!

We argued for a while, on our way to the mall, only the women who passed by was able to take our mind off our constant battle between each other. We shopped and got everything we wanted, but my next stop had to be the food court, I been starving all day and plus I been trying to catch this Lil cutie who work at Popeye's Chicken, she always giving me the eye when I come through the line, I'm gone finally try to shoot my shot, I think it's about time I try to get at her, out the comer of my eye I spot her approaching the counter, I made my way over to her but before I could say anything Lil Rob stepped in my way and spoke, fuck cock block!

Hey what's up baby, how you doing? Lil Rob said cutting his eye at me, while he talked. Hey welcome to Popeye's can I take your order? Not showing him much interest at all. Yea you can if it gone come with your number Lil Rob said.

Why you want my number? She said.

As they made small talk, I began to feel a little jealous, I hated Lil pretty boy mafucka's who liked to throw they looks around, it always made me feel some type of way. Like I really got in my feelings about this girl and I didn't even know her name, like if I don't dig in her, the world is gone end or something. I had to put my shit in check so it didn't show on my face. I mean, I have been chasing her for a while now.

So what's up you and your girls gone slide through my party tonight? Lil Rob Yeah, we gone come through, she said.

The more I looked at her, the more I wanted her and the more he talked to her, the more jealous I got, it sucks to think that I missed my shot but I'll have another one. After we left the mall, I had to go my separate way so I could get all the way fresh for the party tonight, so I hurried home got dressed and I shot straight to Lil Rob house before everybody started showing up, I had to holla at him about some personal business. When I got to the door, before I could knock, the door opened from the other side. Lil Rob pops out with a face of surprise, his body language putting off energy like he trying to hide something, I got curious to my thoughts.

What's up Lil Rob?

What's up with you bro, you here kind of early as hell, I got a couple of stings, I got to put together before the party tonight, Lil Rob said but looking real uneasy like he was hiding something.

Yeah that's all cool, what, you want me to just come back? I just wanted to holla at you about something real quick, I said.

Yeah that's cool but can we talk about it later? He stepped out the door, looking behind him over his shoulder, closing the door behind him.

As a matter of fact, what's up we can holla real quick, what's on your mind?

I wanted to know, how you feel about us making some money together? I said.

That's a stupid question, I'm down with anything that got to do with money. Just tell me what I need to do.

I gave Lil Rob some information, not disclosing all, I didn't know if I could trust us just yet, but we talked a little on the move about Cassie but never said any names, no dates, or even a place or time. I just wanted to fill him out, because at this moment I just needed to know was he on board. One thing I knew for sure is I could not only be the face of this shit, but I was going to use him somehow down the line. He told me he would be willing to hit the move just call him whenever I'm ready, just what I needed to hear, he turned around running back into the door without even saying goodbye, by the way he was acting, that shit made me feel suspicious, so I parked a sit out of view of his house just so I could see who or what he may be hiding inside. It took about two hours before anyone even came to the door but once I seen who came out, it fuckin blew my mind. I was crushed beyond repair I didn't have the words to put together in this situation, I just know I got to be cool, and show no signs like I know anything about this, it makes me wonder, did he know our connection or how long has this been going on damn, he had to know by the way he was acting when he came outside, he was acting real weird, fuck that! I have to know the connect between the two. Well at least I'm not in the dark about It, any more. I got up from my spot I had been hiding and proceeded on to my next place of business, this business was surely done, I was hurt in need of some answers.

Cassie:

This day is turning out to be a crazy one for me, seeing Lamar come up to Robs house like that, I never even knew that they even knew each other. As she stared off into space, she felt a strong guilt come over her for not stepping out, letting him know she was there. Me and Rob is just friends and we been that way for years, but I didn't want Lamar to think nothing crazy, which men tend to do that a lot and I don't need that because I love Lamar so much, even dough we just met, he's special to me, he is the first one I have ever felt this way about and I really want to run away and maybe start a family with him one day. I could really see us together. I haven't told Stacey or anybody about me wanting any of these things, especially about wanting to run away with Lamar, and I rather keep it that way because I don't need no one to try to judge me or even worse, try to stop us, I don't need no one trying to get in our way, damn, damn, damn, I think I even seen Lamar when I was coming out of Robs house, I'm not sure it was him and I could be tripping paranoid, forcing my mind to see things I know isn't really there. Well shit, I hope that isn't there. The thought of Lamar thinking the wrong thing and leaving me is something I couldn't truly stand to bear. As she gets into the car, out of nowhere tears began to start coming down her face beyond her control, she truly didn't do anything wrong but yet she can't figure out why she is so emotional and guilty. When she got to the stop light, she wiped away her tears enough to see her phone was ringing and Lamar was the one calling, she immediately started to panic, wondering if it was him that she seen or what she would say if he did ask was she there at Rob's, she tried to change her pitch in her tone to excitement, so he didn't notice she had just been crying.

Hi baby, she said Hey what's up baby?

Nothing much baby just missing you like crazy!

O is that right huh? So what have you been doing all day, I ain't heard from you all day, you must have been real busy, Lamar said.

At that moment, she wanted to tell him the truth really bad but the words just couldn't roll off the tip of her tongue, but a lie spilled out instead.

I been real busy all day today baby running around with my mom while she paid some bills and we did a Lil shopping, she said but for a minute a strong silence filled up the space on the phone, she didn't know what would be coming next.

Yeah, I been out doing a Lil shopping myself for a Lil party I'm supposed to be going to tonight, at this guy named Lil Rob I know.

Now was the time for her to speak up but instead she let that moment pass her once again.

Ok that sounds like fun, is we gone hook up after you get through with the party, I got some things I want to talk to you about and plus I got a big surprise for you, she said.

You got a surprise for me? Tell me what it is! No! that's why you call it a surprise.

Baby I might be tripping but I swear I saw you earlier when I stopped at my friend Robs house, was that you? Lamar asked searching to see would she tell the truth. The hesitation in her voice spoke its own truth.

Her heart was in her stomach and once again she had another chance to let Lamar know that, that it was her indeed that he seen, but instead once again she took the high road and the choice to tell another lie knowing that it would catch up with her later.

No it wasn't me baby, and if you thought it was me, then why you ain't just say nothing to me when you saw me baby?

Argue began to build in him, because he knew she was lying to him, damn how could she lie to me? I thought that she loved me, was everything she ever said a fuckin lie, he didn't expose his pain, he had to stay focused on the move at hand, that's all that mattered now.

That was the same thing I was thinking, Lamar said.

No baby you just seeing things, damn I didn't know you missed me that much baby but thank you for letting me know, making me feel special. But make sure that we hook up after the party, I really need to see you Lamar, and baby I love you, I got to go so I'll talk to you soon, later bye.

As soon as she hung up, her heart went into her stomach, she knew that he didn't believe her and now no matter how much she might tell the truth, it won't be able to cover up the lie she started with, why was it so hard to just tell the truth.

Lamar:

After I had got off the phone with Cassie I could tell that not only that she was fucking with Rob on the low, hiding it from me when she knew I knew the truth, why wouldn't she just come clean, I really thought she loved me, damn I guess she had me fooled, and with Rob of all people. This shit is crazy, I could aspect it from him but not Cassie, I rolled up a blunt to clear my head, more than half of me is being over powered by the child in me, I began to plot on how I could get revenge and pay the both of them back for the pain that they caused me. I cleaned up my act, then headed to the party before Cassie called, I was into doing a little research of my own, Cassie step dad is a real big shot around town, he been laying down a lot of work and the word is he is not the type to be fucked with, this dude named Jerk I ran with a little bit said he use to work for him here and there until he got his money right and he was planning on putting the play down on him because he knew the ends and outs to his business. He told me at one point at a time they were real close up he cut Jerk out on a big deal and that's when the tables turned on they friendship. I never spoke, I just played a big listener to the conversation, I didn't want to put my plans in the air for someone to grab them or even get wind, this nigga talks to damn much, but thank God for that because ir'he didn't I wouldn't know what I know now. Turns out Cassie step dad name is Joe-John, he use to run around with May-so back in the days and come to find out once he got up in life he didn't even look back May-so way, and that's fucked up.

Don't look out for the people who even look out for you, real disrespectful if you ask me. I knew this was something I knew I couldn't tell May-so about, just because I didn't know how he would take it, being that he put game in the dude like he been doing me! I figure I'm just gone keep this my little secret. Since I know the guy is the type who don't fuck around, once I make a move on this dude I better be playing for keeps. The main thing for me is I didn't want Cassie to find out it's me. I pulled back up to the party and it was thick as hell, fine Lil honey's was everywhere, it seems like the whole hood was in the building. As soon as I came through the door, I had love coming from everywhere, I saw Mike D in the back with his brother Lil Will and two Lil fly honey's shaking they ass all over them, this looked like this could turn into a porno real quick, blunts was rolled up everywhere, you could hardly see through the room it was so much smoke, I got me a drink and just chilled out and hollered at a couple random people that slid through the party, but the whole time I was looking for Lil Rob, I haven't seen him since earlier, after I waited a while longer, I took it upon myself to search the house looking for him, it took a while to find him, which I almost didn't until I was lead to the garage by the sound of moaning, I rounded the corner and out of nowhere a anger grew inside of me, I wouldn't know what to do if I see him fucking Cassie, damn what if it was her, as I got closer I could see Lil Rob digging in the Lil chick from the food court in the mall, pounding her as hard as he can, while she holds on for her dear life to the wall, looking back at him, with a pleading look in her eyes, only for a moment I was turned on, damn she is so beautiful, but then a jealousy filled my body, taking my once hard dick to a very soft one, then hate came after, who the fuck do this motherfucker think he is, he stole her from me and I wasn't tripping, it was cool, but Cassie is a different story. I wanted to kill his ass right here, as I look at him, I wonder what they see in him and it also makes me wonder what they didn't see in me. I watched him deliver every stroke, all the way to the end. All I know is I have to hurt him the way he has hurt me; I just don't know how I'm going to do it just yet. The worst enemy you can have is the one you can't see, after they cleaned up and left, I went to the very spot that he stood, I wanted to stand in the place he stood while he fucked the bitch that was supposed to be mine, I tried to get a hold of my thoughts, give this hurt no power but I couldn't, so I left the party, from the way I was feeling I couldn't face Lil Rob like this, I wanted to hurt him to bad, I had to get my feelings in order, on my way to the house I remembered that Cassie had wanted me to come over, so I called a couple times before I got her to answer.

Hello,

She sounded as if she was asleep, and I had waking her out of a good dream.

What's up baby? I thought you wanted me to come over tonight? You sound like you sleeping!

No I'm not sleep and I do, I just got out the shower, when you get here just come on in, the door will be unlocked, she said.

Damn so where is your parents? Don't have me opening doors and getting shot at and shit!

Baby ain't nothing gone happen to you, I told you already that they gone be gone all night, so wC got the place all to our self so we can chill.

All night huh? Ok I'm about to pull up in a minute ok.

Ok.

We got off the phone, I headed straight to her house. When I pulled up to the front of the house, it seems like all the lights was out, until I opened the door and there were candles lit everywhere. It looked like a romantic scene from the movies. The scent of coco butter filled the air and she had on a real soft jazz song playing at a real nice level, it was just enough to grab your attention as soon as you enter the room. Then I saw Cassie coming down the stairs, she was oiled up real good and all I could think was damn, she had me, I didn't see myself going anywhere any time soon, when she got to the bottom of the stairs she grabbed me by the hand and lead me back up the stairs.

Damn baby where are you taking me? I said searching for the answer in her eyes. You already know where we going.

O is that right, and you ready for this baby?

Yes, Lamar, I thought about it and I truly love you, I want

you to be my first, everything about you, about us is special and I want to show you just how much I truly care about you.

As we walk into the bedroom, I let her undress quickly, then I laid down on the bed and watched her come up out of her clothes slowly, I was turned on by just how beautiful she truly was, she is covered in a pure dark chocolate skin, with the pinkest little middle I have ever seen, her body was perfect, I would change a thing about her, at this moment I felt like the luckiest man in the world. As she came closer, I pulled her down on top of me and we began start kissing passionately I rolled her over and opened her up for a taste, I took long licks, making sure I get every drop of her love, as she moaned, I could tell I was all the way in control, I dipped my tongue inside her tight like hole.

Damn baby you feel so good, she said as she pulled on the back of my head guiding me in every direction I should go. I didn't want to stop I was in love, with her taste, her body, her soul, and all of them was driving me crazy right now. I rolled her over to try to enter her from the back, she stopped me.

No Lamar,

Huh what, I said checking to see if I did something wrong.

I never did this before I want you to get on top baby and please don't hurt me, she said with pleading eyes.

I climbed on top of her and began to try to enter her, forcing myself inside of her but it was hard to break down her walls, she moved from left to right as if she was in pain.

Baby it hurts, please slow down.

It took a little work but I finally had a break through, and her walls wrapped around me like a blanket on a new born baby, damn I got weaker and weaker inside her by the minute, as she held onto me tight, we stared into each other eyes, kissing, enjoying every moment, we weren't fucking, no! this had to be what making love feels like. From there she got comfortable to perform every position you can think of. We fucked all night long I came what had to be a hundred times. She even tried to suck the dick, I stopped her because she wasn't good at that at all, I started to tell her she needed to get some pointer from Stacey but I knew that would only get me in trouble, so I just laughed that off to myself, I didn't want to fuck up the moment. Once we were done we both just laid in the bed sweaty and tired Cassie rolled over into my arms and looked at me.

I want you to know that I love you and I want to kind of ask you a question, she said as we lay there face to face, I could see she had a seriousness in her eyes.

What is it baby? I asked but wondered was this the time that she was going to come clean about lying to me and being at Lil Rob house. I loved her, so now would have been the right time, I would of forgave her in a heartbeat.

If we made enough money baby would you run away with me.

I didn't mean to laugh but I couldn't help it, yea, and then what? We're just going to go live happily ever after huh?

Lamar I'm serious, I really care about you, as a matter of fact I have never felt this way about anybody before. She said with almost tears in her eyes. You could see she had a strong truth in her eyes but what kept bothering me the most is that there just was so many lies that laid in the dark, I wondered if she was trying to play me like a fool, I really wanted to believe her but I know what I saw with my own eyes and that shit hurts.

O you care about me huh? I wanted to tell her what I knew but I just couldn't and why should I, she didn't.

Her facial expression changed with my words of doubt about her and she instantly became angry and impatient with me.

Why you say it, like you don't believe me or something she said searching my eyes for an answer.

I wanted to tell but I kept throwing it off, I knew it would only mess up things if I told her what I saw, it would only put a space between us and that I didn't need right now, so I did what any man would do, I fought a question with a question.

Do you really want to be with me and only me?

She set up in the bed, looking deeply in my eyes as if she couldn't tell a lie and said that's what I just said didn't I?

Even dough I knew she lied to me, I just wasn't ready to give up on her, she is special to me and it just feels really good just to be with her, but a feeling is what it is, a feeling, but the truth shell always set you free and I am, free from being controlled by the feeling.

Yea it is what you said, but I just want you to show me a Lil more that you really want to be with me and that you love me, I said trying not to keep an eye contact.

So what giving you my virginity ain't enough? Damn ok, so how am I supposed to do that?

I want you to put me in position with your step dad, see if he would let me get some money with him.

Lamar I don't know if I could do that, he always tells me to stay out of grown folk's business, he is not going to listen to me, he thinks I'm just a child, he doesn't even know I talk to boys at all, and if he finds out he might flip.

Baby all you got to do is link me up with him and the rest is history.

If he finds out that I like you and you want to sale for him, he won't want mC around you and I don't want that, she said with a strong look of concern in her eyes.

No baby, nothing or nobody is going to ever be able to keep us apart.

I grabbed her up in my arms and held her tight, I knew I couldn't push any more, this would have to be something I would have to work on at a later date but for now I have I wanted to make love to her one more time before I had to get up and go meet up with Lil Rob, he had hit my line in the middle of me and Cassie love making and told me it was important he holler at me and I ain't gone lie, it was kind of weird that he wants me to come alone, so before I go to meet up with him, I made it my business I went to grab my strap, I don't have no time for nobody to get the upper hand on me, it's just something about this meet up, that just don't feel right. Me and Lil Rob have known each other for a while now and we have never had bad blood but you can never be too careful. You can never tell when the love is lost, hell, over my bitch I was ready to kill him earlier. I think what made everything weird and keeps playing in my head is why do he keep telling me that I got to come alone, so because of that I don't know what to aspect from this fool. I parked a couple blocks away from his house, just to make sure nothing crazy was waiting outside for me, as I was walking up to the door Lil Rob was coming out the door to stand on his porch, where we met up, I watched not only my surrounding but his every move as well.

What's up Lil Rob, what was so important you had to talk to me about?

Lil Rob motioned for me to be quiet and to come into the house. When we entered the house, Lil Rob went into the basement and headed straight to the closet. While I was behind him I had my hand on my strap the whole time just in case he tried to pull something funny. When he went inside he pulled out a large black duffel bag and threw it at my feet.

What is it, I asked.

Open the damn bag and take a look!

When I looked into the bag, there were four brinks of heron, strong as fuck, so I could tell that it was pure and uncut.

Damn Lil Rob where did you get this from? I asked surprised that he could come up with this pure of dope being who I knew him to be.

I hit a nice Lil lick on this dude from the hood. What hood? I asked looking for a lead.

That don't matter, the only thing that matters are don't nobody know but you and me. I need some help to get rid of all this shit, I have never sold any of this shit before so I don't even know where to start, have you ever fucked with it?

Yea, I sold a Lil bit of it here and there, I said in confidence I could move it. Good that's why I called you, I figured you would be the best man for the job.

Yea we can make a lot of money off this shit, just give me enough of it so I could let people try it out around town, then once we lock them in, this shit will move fast I know a lot of people, so don't do or tell anybody anything, I'll take care of this for us, you just need to lay low, the less people that know about this, the better.

I was surprise by just how much Lil Rob actually trust me, but then again it could be from the guilt of him messing with my girlfriend behind my back, who knows, all I know is I love money in any and every form that comes my way. After I got what I need from Lil Rob I left and headed home to get me some rest from a long day.

When I wokC up, I could see I had a couple of missed calls from my dad. We been getting really close lately over the last couple of weeks. I can't wait until he comes home from prison so we could finally get to hang out, we are just a like in so many ways. But there are still so many unanswered questions I need answered and he is the only one who can fill that void. I got some plans for me and him, we can take over the game, he could be the missing piece to the puzzle to taking my business in the streets to the next level. He's my dad so I know he would never hurt me and at the same time he can see that I'm ready and that I ain't just some kid out here, I really held it down since he been gone. But it's cool, my dad is back now and we can do this together. In a lot of our conversations we had on the phone, my dad was worried about coming home and getting on his feet, so I'm going to surprise him with a Lil bread to slow down his worry, I really need him focused on the bigger picture, he doesn't need to be stressed over money, when we got a lot of catching up to do. As I continue down my call log, I could see I missed a couple of calls from Mike D and a couple from Cassie as well, plus one from Stacey, damn I must been sleeping real good to sleep through all these calls, Stacey probably want me to slide through this morning, the thought of that put a smile on my face instantly, me and Stacey always have fun when we together, so I hurried up and got in the shower I had not yet washed Cassie off of me from our love making last night, then I got dressed, even dough I wanted to go see Stacey, I can't, I have to go see Mike D to bring him up to date on what I need him to do next.

When I got to Mike D house, Lil Will was at the kitchen table bagging up dime bags of weed, it was crazy to see how fast he had picked up on the hustle. One thing May-so would say is it ain't no telling what a man would do when it comes to some money. I could truly say I know that first hand, I love the chase for money, it's just that so far, I haven't had to run long or far for it.

What's up Lil Will, I see you out chasing a bag early, I said with a little sarcasm in my voice.

What the fuck is you talking about, I ain't out chasing nothing, I'm in here bagging up the bag, he said not catching on to what I said at all.

Dummy, I was just saying I see you hustling now.

Hell yea, a mafucka got to do something, ain't nobody gone give me shit, he said.

So when the hell was you gone tell me you had it poppin, shit I might even want to join you and get some of that money with you? I said with a slight smile on my face.

Yea ok mafucka, you don't even hustle but somehow you do always keep money in yo pocket, I'm starting to think you a damn trust fund baby or something and I better not find out you go stay in a house on the hills when you leave the hood either Lil Will with a serious face.

Lol yea I wish, I ain't coming to visit the hood for fun, where is Mike D at? I asked He in the room, he said motioning me to the back.

When I walked into the room, Mike D was sitting in the corner of the room high as hell, playing the video game talking shit to the screen as if it can hear him.

What's up with you bro, don't tell me all you do is sit on yo ass and play this game all day. Why you ain't out there helping Lil Will bag that damn weed up into dime bags? Instead of wasting your time doing this shit, you could be chasing that money.

Because that shit ain't no real money and for where I'm trying to go and for what I'm trying to do, man that shit would take forever. That shit that my brother doing is pocket change.

Bro something is better than nothing, and you got to start somewhere.

Yea and I will, start on top that is what I'm on, what's up with the move? We setting up Cassie step dad or what.

I'm still putting some of the pieces together, but what if we don't go through with the robbery?

What do you mean, what if we don't go through with the robbery? Man what's going on Lamar? Bro I need that money, shit, we need that money, so we can move up. We can't keep walking around being broke ass nigga's bro, I'm damn near ready to make a move on anybody that get in my way.

The look in his eyes showed me that he meant every little word that he said and more.

The reason I said we probably shouldn't go through with

the robbery is because we might have a better chance of trying to work for him, maybe he will put us on and we can serve the city.

Man bro, don't be foolish, don't keep his circle tight I don't see him fuckin with two kids trying to come up, Lamar tell the truth, is it because you catching feelings for Cassie? Is that why you trying to back out on me now?

As crazy as it seems, I really didn't know how to answer that question. What he said hit my heart but there is not a doubt in my mind on what I want to do, I could see things clear, and the truth is, yea I do love Cassie and would love to spend a life time with her, but money rules the world and the wrong love will strip you naked, so I'm fighting between the two, it's putting me between a rock and a hard place, making it hard for me to know what to do, so I lead with my pride.

Damn so you trying to say I'm stuck over a bitch, that I suggest to you we hit the lick on in the first place because of her big mouth, I said.

Yea I hear you, Mike D said almost as if he was fanning me off. You got to do more than hear me, I said.

Shit could change overnight and you been playing house for a while now, y'all don't be acting like boyfriend and girlfriend, you act more like husband and wife, Mike D said.

Man fuck you, I can't just rush this shit, we don't have any room to make no mistakes, any wrong moves and we can get fuckin killed, dude real known in the streets.

I don't want to sit back and miss out on this money either.

There was nothing left to say, I shook his hand and headed to the door. Some of what he was saying was right, I do have to make a decision soon, on my way out the door my phone started ringing from an unknown number I have never seen before. I usually don't answer but for some reason I felt this call might be important.

Hello, what's up who is this? Hey what's going on son?

Dad, is that you?

Yea it's me, how are you?

I'm well, how are you calling me from an outside number you got a cell phone in there?

They let me out early and I wanted to know can we meet up, I want to kick it with you for a Lil bit, he said with a long pause, waiting for me to answer.

This call was the one I for sure not expecting but it is right on time, now I could start bringing my dad slowly into the business and we together can start to take over the streets.

Yea that's cool, where do you want to meet up at?

Meet me downtown in about an hour, that will givC me time to meet up with my probation officer to let him know what I got planned for the week, because that's something I have to do now and plus I got to put a couple things together real quick it shouldn't take long.

Do you have to do that, you know, check in?

Yea, or they can send me back to prison and lord knows I can't go back to that damn place, he said taking a deep breath.

Naw we don't want that, I need you out here, we got a lot of work to do out here.

I could tell those words made him want to tune in even more.

O yea like what?

Don't worry about that right now, we have more than enough time to sit down and put things together. But first let's upgrade your style of dress, you been down for a minute, so I know you don't know what in and what's out old man, I can't have you running around looking like a member from the 70's show, I said.

Ok, I see you got jokes huh, Lol, son I got a little money but not enough to be out here on a shopping spree.

Pop don't worry about none of that I got you, I got a little money saved up, I could get you together.

Silence filled the phone, he had become lost for words, so I stepped in to kill the void. Pop we good, just take care of your business and I'll see you in an hour.

Ok son, I'll see you soon.

After we got off the phone, I rushed home to put some money together for my dad, I were going to give him $5,000 but figure $20,000 would get him comfortable enough to the point of no worry, I needed him to be focused for my next move.

When I got downtown in the mall, I met my dad in the food court where I was crushing on that Lil chick Lil Rob fucked, a part of me still wanted to shoot my shot but I didn't I don't play second well. I went and grabbed something to eat before we went shopping. I want to talk to him and wrap my head around his plans before I told him mines, when we sat down I could tell he had something on his mind, so in order to clear it, I slid him the bag of money out of nowhere and when he opened it up, his eyes opened up real wide.

O my God son, where did you get all this money?

I didn't answer, I just smiled and continued to eat my food. He began to get nervous like we had just robbed a bank and needed to find a getaway plan.

Dad relax everything is ok, we ain't got to hide from nothing, I ain't do nothing wrong!

In my mind I was thinking, well at least not today, I don't think I could tell him the truth about me just yet, I don't know what he would do or how he would even take that information, that type of information just ain't for everybody.

Where did you get all this money son? He asked searching my eyes for an answer.

I been working hard, doing a couple jobs here and there for a friend and making a couple of investments to keep money flowing I said not sharing eye contact with him.

At twelfth son, you doing jobs for friends and making investments, he said with a strong look of disbelief.

No I'm thirteen and yea I'm telling the truth, why you acting like you don't believe me?

Whatever, I wasn't thinking about no shit like that when I was your age, let alone had access to this much money and I know if you gave me this much money like it ain't nothing, then you have to have more.

He was looking for an answer I couldn't give, so I just did my best to change the subject, because I wanted to move me off the topic list.

Dad I'm glad you home, but I can't say the same about mom I think she really hates your guts! Well that shit ain't nothing new, me and your mom haven't got a long for a while now.

Even dough I changed the subject I could see in his face he was still searching for more, we went shopping and talked a little more about the future but anytime I asked him about the past, he would say son just let the past be the past and I understand everybody has secrets, I mean, I have a lot of secrets of my own, but there are a lot of things I need answered to be able to move forward with my dad. And by him not willing to answer a lot of my questions, he gave me a real funny feeling inside. After we left the mall, me and my dad split up, I was tired and had a long day with him. I just wanted to go home and get me some rest, put all my thoughts to rest. My mind had been running a race all day. I wonder why my dad didn't want to talk about his past or if he was really hiding something, all I know is only time will tell, the truth always comes out.

When I got to the house, I settled in for the night, I ate and took a shower, then popped in a movie and prepared myself to go to bed to get ready for another day, then out of nowhere my phone rang, when I answered Cassie sounded like she was in a panic almost as if she had got robbed or did the robbery herself and needed a getaway driver.

Baby listen to me, you have to come get me, she said with worry in her voice. Hold up baby, what's wrong?

I need you to come get me right now, hurry baby come on.

Baby I need you to calm down and let me know what's going on, what happen? Did somebody hurt you? Because if!

No, no baby, I took a lot of stuff from my step dad for us baby and I have to get it out of here before he realizes it's either gone or that I took it, baby he's going to kill me if he finds out I took it.

Baby why?

I thought you said we was going to be together and that we were going to run away together, that you love me, you wanted me to show you have much I truly love you and now here it is.

Baby I do love you and all of those things are true, I am going to run away with you but what if your step dad finds out we did all this?

He is going to find out but it won't matter baby, because we will be long gone by then. I don't care if he finds out I just want to be with you that's all that matters to me, she said.

Where would we go, I asked searching for my questions to be answered on the spot.

We can go anywhere baby, it's a lot of money in this bag and a lot of weed also to make more, so tell me is you with me or not, I already did what I did, I can't put it back, damn I can't turn back now!

Yes, baby, I'm with you, just let me get a ride but don't worry I'll be there soon, just try to calm down.

Ok, baby I'm waiting on you.

And baby don't tell nobody about this, this is just between you and me and baby I love you, I said.

I won't I promise and Lamar I love you too I really do, she said with so much promise in her voice.

When we hung up, I sat for a minute, but I can't lie my mind was blown on what she had just done, I did not aspect her to do this, but now I know what my momma meant when she would say to me all the time, love will make you do some crazy things. I got back on the phone after I put my plan in motion,

I called Lil Rob to see if he could get a ride to go get Cassie for me. I wanted to see if they could still hide what they were doing behind my back in my face.

Hello,

Hey Lil Rob I need you to do me a big favor, I said smiling inside.

And what the hell might that be, I was just about to go to bed man, he said in his iratest voice.

I'm tied up at the house big time, I got the dude coming to meet me to take a look at our business we got together, he said if everything right, he gone buy all of them from us as early as tomorrow morning, so I can't leave I don't want to miss him, but I need you to get a ride and go pick up my girl Cassie for me bro, I really need this favor.

It was a long pause then he finally answered, you want me to go pick your girl up and take her where Lamar?

I need you to bring her to my house, like I said I'm tired up here and this shit is for the both of us, bro we need this money, this shit could be big, look if I really didn't need you I wouldn't called.

Damn Lamar, ok I got you, but you owe me, he said with anger in his voice. Damn you making money ain't enough, I laughed then ended the call.

When I hung up, all I could do was shake my head. I was just so amazed how he could act like they ain't been fuckin around behind my back and I wonder will he have the nuts to even tell me to my face what's been going on. I had no time to let these thoughts take over my mind, even dough it really hurt my heart I had to get up and get dressed and figure out what was about to happen next.

Lil Rob & Cassie:

When Lil Rob pulled up to Cassie house, he wondered why Lamar had him really pick Cassie up. Was he telling the truth about meeting the guys to show them the shit or was he thinking something was going on between them and wanted to get them face to face to confront them. He had never asked him to do anything like this before, maybe thinking I was going to try to get on with them or something but I would never do that to him. Why ask me of all people, he could of asked Mike D that's his best friend, not me, and he been acting real funny every since I had the party at my crib. I hope he didn't see Cassie coming out my house earlier that day and think that we been fucking behind his back, he the type to think like that too. Me and Cassie been friends since we were little kids, my parents and her parents are best friends. I have never even looked at her that way; she is more like a little sister to me more than anything. I just don't know why she hasn't told him that shit yet. When Cassie came outside to get in the car, I could tell she was real surprised to see me, she was carrying two large duffel bags like she was either moving out or not planning to come back for a while. When Cassie opened the door, she looked all around for Lamar only seeing me, made her even more confused.

Lil Rob what are you doing here? And where is Lamar? He is the one who is supposed to be coming to get me.

Calm down, I'm just doing him a favor, he said he was tied up taking care of some business so he asked me to come get you.

How did he know you even know where I live? Did he give you the address?

It had not donned on him that he didn't offer her address or anything and I never asked, things was beginning to get more and more weird.

I don't know but Cassie I think we should tell him we been friends since we were little kids so he doesn't start thinking something different.

Look we are going to tell him, this is just not a good time right now, she said bursting him off.

What do you mean not a good time, you really make it seem like we got something going on between us, like we got something to hide Cassie! I don't want to fall out with this guy because he thinks I'm doing his girl behind his back.

Believe me, I know Lamar, if he thought that we were fuckin around he would have said something by now.

How you know he ain't just waiting on you to come clean with the truth and what's going on, why is you leaving in the middle of the night with those big ass bags? What's in them?

Lil Rob reached for one of the bags so he could have a look inside one of them but got his hand smacked along the way.

Stop being nosey! And do what you were sent here to do and that's give me a ride, not be in my business. If it's something I wanted you to know I'll tell you!

O so it's like that huh?

Yea it's like that, you my best friend not my man or my dad, I don't have to tell you everything.

Lil Rob knew how Cassie could get when she got upset so he just rode in silence the whole ride to Lamar house but his thoughts were eating at him, what was in the bags and why wouldn't she talk to him. Damn was she planning on running away. He had to push one more time to see would she be willing to open up to him.

Cassie, I know I'm not your man or your dad or anything but I'm not just a friend, I'm your best friend and if you don't tell me something I'm going to be worrying myself sick about you, he said with so much concern in his eyes, I kind of made her feel bad, but she promised to Lamar that she would tell.

You don't have to worry about me, I'm a big girl Rob.

But I am going to worry about you, so tell me what's going on, is you running away from home and if so why?

Cassie looked Lil Rob in his eyes as he pleaded with her for the truth, she dropped her head, she made a promise to Lamar she wouldn't say nothing about what she done and she wasn't going to break it for no one, she loved him just that much, but she also knew she just could say nothing.

Her mom and step dad would go looking for her and Lil Rob house would be the first place they would look.

Me and my mom got into a fight and I'm just going to stay with Lamar for the night to let things cool off a little bit, if you must know she said, twisting her neck at Lil Rob.

You got two big bags packed to go spend a night, tell the truth Cassie, because that shit you saying ain't adding up! I think it's a lot more to the story.

They pulled up in front of Lamar house but refused to let her leave without an answer that made sense, locking the doors and holding on to her arm, in action like her big brother, trying to talk her into not making the wrong choice.

There is no more to the story that's it and I packed extra clothes just in case I have to stay out longer and if that happens more than likely I'll go stay at Stacey house or somewhere else if you tell my parents where I'm at.

He let her go but before she left out the car, she gave him a hug to assure him that everything was going to be ok.

Lamar:

I saw Lil Rob and Cassie pull up to my house and what was crazy is I never even gave him an address to where she lives or a phone number for him to even try to get in touch with her but yet he never asked either, messy! It was becoming more and more obvious that they been fuckin around for a while now and what hurts is why me? She doesn't have to lie to me, if she wants to be with him, then be with him, she doesn't have to cheat on me. The more I thought about them being together, the angrier I got, the more I felt betrayed, the more I wanted them to feel the pain that I was feeling and while I was looking out the window into the car, I just seen Cassie and Lil Rob in what looks to be fighting over something, but what could they be fighting over, a part of me wants to go outside and confront the both of them together, they them know that I know what's going on, but what would that do? All they are going to do is lie and I'll just look like a fool. Then out of nowhere while I was still glued to the window, I saw Cassie reach over and give him a hug and kiss, what the fuck is going on, is the only thoughts that came to my mind, I couldn't help it, I ran to go put on my shoes to go outside but before I could get out the door, Cassie was already there at the door knocking, I needed answers and she was only going to get one more chance to answer them. I opened the door fixing my face, I couldn't let her know that I know about her and him, all I can hope is that she will tell me the truth before I end up doing something stupid. As soon as the door open she ran into my arms and a flood of kisses followed, how could she kiss me after she kissed him, nasty bitch, she probably sucked his dick on the way over here, damn what should have been a moment of happiness was overpowered with so many fucked up thoughts, thoughts of them fuckin, thoughts of her sucking his dick and then coming to fuckin kiss me, playing me like a fuckin fool, I took a step back to put some space between us to look her in the face, I always felt like the eyes can't tell a lie. When the kisses stopped, the questions started.

Is something wrong baby? She said looking into his eyes as he moved away like something was bothering him.

How could she ask a question like that, knowing damn well she knew what was wrong, the more I looked at her I felt like my head was going to explode.

Nothing wrong baby, I was just almost sleep so I got to wake back up that's all.

Baby don't worry I'll wake you up, I'm here now, she said with the biggest smile on her face I have ever seen.

O is that right?

Yea, that's right!

Why don't we get the bags put away so we can go take a walk and talk about what's next for us, I said.

Why can't we just chill here and talk baby it is kind of late?

Because I'm trying to smoke and chill baby, maybe have a couple drinks and shit, I don't want my mom all nosey in my business knowing you here, you know I got to sneak you in, but most of all I want to talk about us.

What about us? She said wondering where he was leading too.

I just want to make sure, you sure about us, and us running away together and shit I don't want you changing your mind on me, because that would really hurt me.

Baby I'm not going nowhere I love you, she said looking dep into his eyes not looking away, not even for a second.

Ok well look, it's just things that's been on my mind we should talk about but we can't do it here because you get loud when you get excited and I don't want you waking my momma and her boyfriend up getting us busted.

Lollook at you, always being nasty Lol she said while shaking her head walking away.

After we got everything settled we headed out to our favorite Lil spot in the park by the river I used my mother car while she was sleep so I 'll have it back before she even notices that it's gone. Cassie loves this park, she would always say it's because of how the lights reflect off the water at night, me, I just needed a quiet place to talk. When we set down we had a couple of drinks and shared a lot on what we want in our future together and everything sounded great but I have to know if she is cheating on me with Lil Rob before we can truly move forward, not knowing for sure is eating me alive.

Baby I been wanting to ask you a question all night that's been eating at me and it's very important to me, so please don't lie to me.

She looked like a child, at this moment who was in trouble by her father. I'm not going to lie to you, what is it baby?

Do you love me?

Yes,

Do you really care about me? Yes,

Baby have you been cheating on me this whole time we been together, Cassie don't lie to me. No baby why would you say that, what would make you think that?

Because I saw you in Lil Rob hugging and kissing before you got out the car, you could have just told me you were fuckin him, you didn't have to lie to me.

No baby I mean yea I hugged him I didn't kiss him and hell no I'm not fuckin him! Yet! Is that what you telling me?

No me and Lil Rob is friends, we been friends since we were little kids, there ain't nothing going on between us.

Your lying to me, why didn't you just tell me that shit instead of sneaking behind my back cheeping out his house and shit, lying about it.

Baby I was going to tell you, but I didn't know how you would take it.

The more she lied to me, I could feel the anger and the rage inside me taking over and before I knew it, I punched her in the face, the first one making her fall to the ground, as I walked toward her, I could see a fear cover her face, she began to plead for me to stop, but it only fell on deaf ears I only wanted to unleash the pain on her that she had did to my heart, I climbed on top of her in one motion, piiuiing her down with my hand around her throat, punching and choking her until no motion was left in her body once she stopped breathing I realized I had went too far but still in my actions, I felt I didn't go far enough, Lil Rob had to pay as well, so I pulled out the used condom he had used to fuck the girl on the side of the house at the party to put inside of Cassie so she could be filled with his DNA if she wasn't already, plus so she could get the justice she so deserve for this tragic crime against her. I found a broken broom stick in the wooded area by the river and fucked her with it until I could see the blood drip off the tip. When I was done and in full satisfaction of healing my pain, I walked away looking over my shoulder, feeling no regret, as I got to the top of the hill, I could hear moans and groans coming from the wooded area I just left, damn she was still alive after everything I did. At that point I wished I could change what happen but now it's too late, I'm in to deep and have to finish the job. I admired how strong she truly was but that would be no match for me, I was so much stronger. I walked back to the place where she was laying and just watched her choke on her own blood and fight to get a word out and once she did, I knew every day after this one, her words would haunt me for the rest of my life.

Lamar (choking sound) Lamar (choking sound) please don't, don't do this! She said showing real signs of pain.

My heart had hurt from the sight of her and thinking about what she did to me only made me hate her even more, I have no mercy for her, fuck her, just like she had no mercy for me, as I approached her closer, she began to try to kick as hard as she could, begging for her life and asking why, I couldn't help but to answer.

Why, you ask why! Because you played me, why, because you were fuckin one of my boys behind my back, lying to my face, thinking you was going to get away with it, why, because I loved you and you broke my fuckin heart, shit, I gave you every chance in the world to just make shit right, but you didn't! no you didn't!

Before I left the house, I had filled a needle with the pure uncut heron that Lil Rob gave me, to test and build customers but now with everything going on I am deciding to use it on her instead, feel her veins with it, like she filled my heart with lies, she started fighting hard once she seen the needle, making it hard for me to be able to stick any of her vain, so I stabbed her over and over again until the needle was empty, I could see the drug taking effect, by the slowness in her movement and her eyes started to roll to the back of her head. Once again I had fallen into a strong stage of rage, and by her not having enough strength to scream, gave me more confidence I had more time with her, I had to have more time with her, to truly end this love affair. I took the rest of the heron I had and crushed the bag, pouring it into her mouth and down her throat, then I cover her mouth until she could no longer fight any more, tears roll down her face as her life slowly slip away. She was overdosing hard and fast, there was nothing left in her to give.

When it was over I kissed her on the cheek and wiped her tears away. I stayed to the end, after she died, I stayed with her as long as I could. I knew in my heart, I was going to miss her, she was my first love but in the end it's always business over bullshit, besides her cheating on me with Lil Rob, I had to cut my ties. Only in a perfect world we could of ran off together and lived happily ever after. But this is the real world and in the reality of things, Cassie step dad is a powerful man in the streets and it wouldn't be hard to connect the dots and connect me to her. I know the love for a daughter is forgivable when they make mistakes, me on the other hand would not be that lucky. I know he would kill me in a heartbeat. It came down to me choosing her or the money, so I took the money, even dough I loved her. The ride home was hard, I just kept picturing her face and the fear in her eyes, I had to keep myself together just in case people would come questioning me about her and not just that this was only one part of the job that need to be finished. When I got home I cleaned myself off really good by taking a bleach bath and didn't waste no time putting together my next part of my plan, at this point I knew time was of the essences and I had no time to waste. I counted all the money that Cassie had stolen and brought me, it came up to a little over 250,000.00 dollars in cash and 50 pounds of weed. What I noticed about the money is it was wrapped in a certain way only her step dad could tell the difference, this was something that I could use to my advantage, even dough I knew it was late, I knew Lil Rob would not turn down no money so I called him and he agreed to meet up with me at his house. When I came in the house I could tell he wanted to question why I was there and where was Cassie, why did I come alone and I answered every question in my own way. Before I exposed the real reason I was there, I showed my interest in how he committed the robbery to get the heroin, we laughed and joked about the details, then I got down to business.

Lil Rob that heroin is fire, I been passing it out to everyone all over town and now my phone won't stop ringing, I said drawing him in with every word.

I told you that shit was good as hell and I came through for us, now we can really get this money, he said with his arms crossed, shaking his head, showing his confidence in himself.

Speaking of money, I brought you ten bands to get this shit started.

Ten bands! Where did you get all that money from so fast? I just gave you that shit yesterday.

I told you I had some people lined up in the morning, them people just couldn't wait, that's why I'm up trying to get this business took care of now, plus you know that's just how I do thangs, I move fast and it was a lot of people who fronted me the money because the shit was just that good, but listen to me, don't go spending this money real fast, just wait because it ain't no telling if we gone need it to re-up on more dope.

From the look in his eyes, you could tell he hadn't held that much money ever before and if the mall was open tonight, he would be on his way to spend everything he had with no problem, I pressed him for a promise to hold on to the money, until the dope was at least gone and he agreed. I grabbed more of the heroin and headed for the door from there I went home and went straight to bed. The morning felt like the speed of light, the sun poked through the window forcing me to toss and turn to gain comfort, which was coming no time soon. I could hear the news anchor talking about Cassie and how she was found by a jogger, jogging in the park early in the morning. I could picture her being visible to any and everybody as soon as the sun rise hit the river. The way the lady describe the scene was almost like I was learning about everything for the first time myself. Before I knew it the tears rolled down my face in a non-stop motion, hitting my chest before I could wipe them away. I have to get up and get ahead of this thing, I think it's time to go see her step dad so we can have a talk.

Lil Rob:

Last night I could not sleep at all; I was excited about what the morning would bring. I wanted to go shopping so bad but Lamar made me promise to hold on to the money and he was right, I will never have nothing if I'm always spending everything. I need to set myself on the right path so I could shit on all these haters who want to see me down and $10,000 is a good damn start. I turned on the TV to see what the weather will be while I figure out what I was going to eat for breakfast, when I saw breaking news come across the TV screen it got my attention. They started talking about a murder, I wanted to know what was going on, so I hurried up and turned up the volume. The park that the lady was standing at doing her report was me and Cassie favorite park, we been going there since we were kids, she would always force me to go there because she would tell me it's because of the view but now the lady was talking about a girl had got killed last night and found by a jogger, jogging early this morning, I doubt when she finds this out she would want to ever go there ever again. The news anchor describes the scene and it brought chills down my spine.

Damn how could anyone do that type of shit to someone and why? It's plenty of pussy in this world, why in the hell do someone got to take it? That had to be what happen and that's sad.

Then the news talked about how the girl have been identified, then out of nowhere Cassie picture popped up on the TV screen, my heart went into my stomach and I instantly got sick. How in the hell could this happen to her, did Lamar do this and if so why? All I know is he was the last one she was with, so I pulled out my phone to call Lamar I had to get some answers, the phone ring over and over and then he answered.

Hello,

Lamar, what the fuck is going on, I said with anger pouring out of my voice on the call.

What you mean what's going on, I just woke up not too long ago, he said like he didn't know what was going on.

I saw Cassie picture all over the news, she was killed in the park last night and some jogger found her body this morning.

Man quit playing, that can't be Cassie, she went back home last night, he said as if he didn't have a care in the world.

Why! Shit she told me she was going to spend the night with you, I said searching for more answers.

Yea she was supposed to, but we got in a fight last night because when I came to see you about our money move, she thought I snuck out the house to meet some other bitch, I told her I went to meet you but she didn't believe me, so she got mad and left out. When I get off the phone with you I'm gone call her, we gone be good.

Bro she is fuckin dead, ain't no calling her, now tell me what's going on, why did you do it? She was my best friend!

Silence took over the phone at that moment I could tell that Lamar was lost for words, but the next ones sent a chill down my spine.

Fuck you and that bitch, what, you were fuckin her behind my back, now you talking about y'all was best friends, this the first time I heard this shit come out yo mouth, I didn't even know y'all knew each other, from the way you acted.

I had never saw Lamar act like this and to tell you the truth it really bothered me, if he could do this to Cassie I was scared of what he would do next so I hung up on him because I had heard enough and I made a call to the police to tell them what I know, just in case something did happen to me. Now I know I'm supposed to live by the street code and not snitch or even get the police involved at all but fuck that! This is my best friend and besides it being the right thing to do, I just know if the shoes were on the other foot, Cassie would do the same thing for me.

911 what's your emergency?

The girl who got killed in the park, I think I know who did it! Lamar:

Damn, as soon as I heard the phone hang up I knew I fucked up. Why did I say that shit to Lil Rob? As soon as he started talking about him and Cassie being friends, my emotions got the best of me, I thought about him making love to her the way I do behind my back and I snapped.

Those very uncontrollable emotions could be the end of me, I have to get my shit together and make it to Cassie step dad house before he does. I put some of the money in the bag along with the heroin Lil Rob gave me and called my uncle Scottie girl Sharon to give me a ride, I knew I couldn't just go alone. When we pulled up to the house, I could see a lot of cars parked outside, we found a place to park and I threw the bag over my shoulder as me and Sharon both walked to the door of the house. After a couple of knocks at the door Cassie mom answered.

Who is it, she said, with a deep sadness in her voice. It's Lamar ma'am.

When she opened the door and her eyes connected with mine, it was as if her life had been drained from her soul. Her spirit had been broken like a person that had nothing else to live for.

What is it Lamar, it's a lot going on right now!

Ma'am I really am sorry for your lost, I really loved Cassie with all my heart and life is not going to be the same without her.

As I spoke I could feel the tears pouring down my face as I drop my head, Cassie mom reached out and grab me into her, so she could give me a hug, and she hugged me as tight as she could, after our embrace, I looked her in the face and told her it's important that I talk to Cassie step dad, she turned around and lead me right to him. When I got to him, he was sitting on the couch with a picture of Cassie in his hand, his face showing different channels of pain, as I approached him closer, the way he looked at me was almost as if he could look straight through me.

Sir is it ok if I talk to you in private?

Yea, what is it about, he said looking me up and down trying to read me without the words. Sir, I really rather we speak in private, it's very important, I said.

He got up in a real slow pace like ten years was added to his age overnight, as he headed to the basement I followed, as soon as we walked inside he was all business.

Ok what the fuck up Lil nigga! What the fuck you want? He said closing in the space between us.

I opened up the bag and dumped it on the table the closest to us.

I think Lil Rob is the one who killed Cassie! I said looking for his reaction so I know what to do next.

With one look at the money Cassie step dad rushed me, picking me up off my feet as he slammed me up against the wall.

What the fuck is you doing with my money? And don't lie to me because I won't fuckin hesitate to kill you, he said staring deep into my eyes, watching for signs to see if I'm lying.

Lil Rob gave it to me, he told me he robbed somebody and he cut me in on the money if I just sell this heroin for him.

That don't make since, why would he give you money to make money and how did you link it to me'?

The tighter his grip the lesser I could breathe, I had to come up with something quick or he was going to kill me, so I went into my pocket and pulled out the tape recorder and played Lil Rob bragging about a robbery he committed. That was enough for him to loosen his grip, where I could speak on things a little clearer, I knew they would find out that I talked to Cassie last night so I decided to use that to my advantage.

When I talked to Cassie last night, she said Lil Rob was coming to pick her up, I kept asking why, but she wouldn't tell me. Lil Rob called me later on last night saying he had something for me so I went over there because he acted like it couldn't wait till the morning, when I got there Cassie was nowhere in sight, when I asked where she was, he told me they had a fight and she went back home, that sounded funny to me, so when he wasn't paying attention I decided to record the rest of the conversation and that's when he told me about the robbery and gave me this bag. He kept saying over and over this was a fresh start for us if I kept quit.

The more I looked at him, I could tell the wheels started

turning in his head, all of a sudden he put me down then went behind the desk and looked on his computer.

You better not be lying to me or I swear I'll kill yo Lil ass in a heartbeat!

You got to believe me, I ain't lying, I'm just trying to do the right thing, I know Lil Rob is my boy but Cassie didn't deserve this!

What time did you talk to her last?

It was about 10:30 pm after I came in the house from playing basketball with my boy Mike D so it had to be between 10:30 and 11:00 o' clock when he picked her up because we didn't stay on the phone that long, she told me he was waiting outside for her.

By the look on his face I could tell he had found what he was looking for because I could see the rage in his eyes as he grabbed his pistol out his desk and headed my way.

What are you doing, please don't kill me I'm not lying, I said bracing myself for the first shot.

I know, but you are going to kill that son of a bitch for me or I'm gone take it as if you are with him and then I'm just gone kill both of y'all ass.

When he said it, there was a look of fear in my eyes but a sense of relief in my heart, my plan had worked after all, I turned the table.

So what is it going to be? You, him, or the both of y'all, he said with a look as if I said the wrong thing he would just kill me right there.

I spoke up but in a low tone, it's gone be him for sure.

When is it going to be done, because I ain't waiting long this shit got to happen asap. Before the end of the night, you got my word.

Yea, that's what I like to hear, but hey remember, if it's not done tonight, I'll be coming to see you in the morning, and Lamar.

Yes, sir,

Make it messy, I want to see him make the news, I want his momma to feel the same pain I feel.

He turned the gun around and handed it to me, I looked him in the eye one last time before I tucked the gun in my pants and left him in the basement as he was stuck in space with his thoughts. Once I got upstairs I said my goodbyes to Cassie's mom, then me and Sharon headed out the door. When I got in the car, I kept my face pinned to the window. I knew if me and Sharon locked eyes, she would turn the questions on full blast.

Could we turn some music on please, this silence is killing me, I said keeping my eyes to the window.

Are you ok, do you want to talk? You know I'm here for you, she said with compassion in her eyes for my situation. All I could think is if she only knew the truth about all this.

Not really, I really just don't have much to say, I just can't believe that she is gone.

Sharon reached over and touched my hand to comfort me, she always just looks so good to me, the more I looked at her and she touched my hand I could feel my nature rising, I could tell that she noticed too because of the change in her body language, at this moment, I didn't care. My mind and my body, my emotions and my thoughts was all over the place. I have to stay focused I can't focus on her right now, I got a lot of shit ahead of me, she moved her hand back really quick but not before she put a real nasty look on her face.

I see even in a sad or fucked up situation like this, you still could be nasty, you and yo uncle act just the fuck a like, she said shaking her head.

She searched my eyes for an answer, but I had none, I just went back to looking out the window, she wasn't use to me not paying her any attention, I could hear her taking in her deep breath to pull my eyes back to hers but that didn't work either, then out of nowhere she started to caress my thigh, moving slowly to my already hard dick, to make it even harder, I opened up to her touch without even noticing the control she was having over me, I just knew even with my mind all over the place, no or stop was nowhere in my vocabulary, after she let go of my man hood I could feel her going up to my belt line at the same time, she reached over and started kissing me, I opened up even more, I was surprised this was all happening, I had wanted this for a long, long time now, then she stopped and jumped back real quick, about time I opened my eyes to adjust to her movement, she had the gun Cassie step dad gave me in her hand, now all I could think in damn now what!

What the fuck is you doing with this gun? She asked pushing the issue. I need it for my protection! Damn chill Sharon.

Protection from what Lamar? You need to get to talking!

It ain't nothing to talk about, I'm in the streets and you can't act like you don't know what the streets bring if you ain't on point.

I didn't know that, obviously you hide a lot of shit really good from me, but all I know is I love you and I don't want to see you get hurt out here, fuckin with these streets.

What type of love do you have for me?

The look of confusion crossed her face, as she fixed herself, on just how to answer my question, giving me enough time to grab the gun out of her hand.

Just like I thought, don't play both sides of the fence, just keep shit real with me! What do you mean both sides? she said showing real interest in my answer.

Trying to act like my mom one moment and then touching and kissing all on me the next, pick a side and stay there!

She sat back in her seat, lost for words in the moment, as I reached for the door to get out of the CDI.

Lamar wait!

After I shut the door behind me I turned around to look back through the window to see what she had to say.

What Sharon?

Can you come over tonight? So we can talk more about this, and Lamar, all of this needs to stay between us, ok.

She reached over and gave me one last kiss as her way of saying goodbye, I stood and watched as the car drove out of sight. Now that Sharon was gone I had to finish out my mission, the very last thing to make everything complete, which is kill Lil Rob, I reached in my pocket to look for my phone and I couldn't find it, damn I must of left it in Sharon car and I have no way to call her back, damn I have to keep moving forward, I have to get this done or Cassie step dad is going to be after me and ain't no telling what Lil Rob is been up to by now, I have to get him before he runs his mouth all over town or worse, he might go to the police with what he knows. I went into my house to get the rest of the money Cassie brought over, just in case the police do come, I could have a clean house, I don't need nothing laying around that I can't answer for, but the question is, where am I going to take it? I have never been good at lying to my grandmother, plus I know this wouldn't be something she would approve of, once I told her this truth, she would for sure look at me like I'm a monster and she wouldn't be wrong, because a monster is what I have become, without any reason but greed. Once I gathered my thoughts, the only place I could take it to would be Mike D house, I knew once he seen the money he would ask some questions, but be more excited about the money because of the change in his position, that type of shit has always been a part of life. Don't nobody give a fuck, as long as they get a cut. When I got to Mike D house, what I didn't expect was to see Lil Rob leaving out the back door, I watched him as he got into the car with his mom, it made me wonder all the things that have been said, after he and his mom was completely out of sight I walked up to the door and knocked, I threw the duffel bag I had on my back on the ground bracing myself for whatever is going to come next, Lil Rob and Mike D has always been real close and with that, you have to be careful because people will pick a side in a heartbeat, I can't let him rock me to sleep, it's time to see who side he's truly on. When the door opened Mike D ran out and hugged me.

Bro where the hell you been, I been calling and texting your phone, he said with a concern look in his eyes.

Why what's going on? I said acting as if I truly didn't know, playing dumb beats the truth any day.

Lil Rob and his mom came around here asking questions, playing detective and shit! I acted as if I wasn't bothered, but deep down I truly was, this police ass nigga.

So what was the questions they were asking?

They were asking crazy ass shit like did you tell me that you killed Cassie? Would I lie for you and they kept saying you need to do what's right for Cassie, trying to make us witnesses or something. He even told me they had been friends since they were little kids, shit I never heard from him, which is weird being that we been friends since we were little, why keep that a secret? They probably were fucking! He said moving pass me to go into the refrigerator.

I walked in and threw the duffel bag in the closet and then I went to sit down on the couch. So he thinks that I killed Cassie?

Well, yeah, that's what I been trying to tell you and from the way he was talking, I think they was on their way to the police station. I tried to talk him out of it but he wasn't listening to me.

Man I ain't do that shit!

So why he thinks you the one who did that shit then Lamar? Come on now this me baby! You can keep it real with me I ain't gone rat you out.

He probably trying to pin it on me because I confronted

him about them fuckin around behind my back, but I really think he had something to do with it and now he trying to blame it all on me, I said while not sharing eye contact at all.

Hold up wait! Lil Rob and Cassie was fuckin around?

I think so, she never told me they were childhood friends.

I caught myself on the next words, I almost told him what I had seen in the car that night he dropped her off, I got up and made a move to the door, I felt like I had said enough.

Mike D I got to go, I'm just gone holla at you later, I said leaving out the door.

Where you going? We still got a lot to talk about, just hold on I'll roll with you if you need me to, he said trying to get his things n as fast as he can.

I really just need to go somewhere to clear my head, but bro I'm good, I'm just going too caught up with you later.

Mike D searched my eyes to see if I really meant what I just said, once again I avoided eye contact then walked right pass him, I could feel him watching me till I was all the way out of sight, I never looked back, not even once until I hit the comer just in time to see him go back in the house, I know he didn't believe my story it was to many holes in the middle but that was something I would have to deal with later, now I'm on my way to go see Lil Rob to finish this once and for all.

Sharon:

O my God I can't believe what I just done.

Her heart was pounding fast, her thoughts was all over the place and she didn't know what to do next, she really loves his uncle but he is constantly in and out of jail. This is still no excuse but it's been hard dealing with her loneliness.

O my God, what do I do, what do I do, she said.

She is lost in her thoughts about Lamar, it's something about him that turns her on, maybe he reminds her of his uncle or it's just the curiosity taking over her judgement, but all she knew is she had to have him, it's been a long time since she been touched the way she needed to be touched, and she just needed to feel him inside of her, filling up her walls, closing all the empty space, as she sat in her car staring out the window, she also thought about what everybody would think if they found out they was messing around. She had never been a hoe, she has always been a good girl, loyal girl in every relationship she was in, but this was different, she didn't want to be in a relationship with Lamar, she just wanted him to be her dirty little secret, that's if he can keep it between them. She also worried about his age, damn she could get in trouble, but she also knew that he from the streets he would never tell. It hasn't been long and she already wanted to hear his voice, damn the thought of him just makes her mouth water. She wants to text him but leaving crazy messages on his phone would be stupid because they could be read by anybody, damn what am I doing, she thought, but couldn't stop herself, so she decided to call to make sure that he was coming over for sure tonight.

Ring, ring, ring!

As soon as the phone started ringing in her ear, she could hear a loud ringing coming from the passage side of the car.

Damn he left his phone in the car, she reached over and picked it up.

She wondered if he had been trying to call his phone to see where it was and she hadn't heard him call at all because of the loud music she had been playing all the way home. She didn't want to be nosey but she had to check his messages, it drove her crazy on whether she should look in his phone or not.

It was like a monkey was sitting on my back beating me over the head, putting a stronghold on my attention, what's on his phone?

Lamar:

About the time I got to Lil Rob house, I was irritated, I took a lot of different routes just so I wouldn't be seen by anybody going to or coming from his house or the surrounding houses. Man I just wanted this to be over with, I knew this wouldn't be easy, there is a lot of front streets that lead to open roads, but I have to do what I have to do. As soon as I made it to the house, I noticed that not a soul was home. So instead of hiding in the bushes, I thought why not look for the spare key and that way I could wait inside the house for them to come home. I want to close in the space they had to get away, I would wait until they became relaxed, then do what I came to do. I could not afford no mistakes, I can't leave no witnesses, I have to tie off all loose ends, or it was going to be the end of me. I just kept playing everything in my mind over and over again, to the point I was starting to become more and more restless. I couldn't get a good taste out of my food, so I started eating less and less until I just stopped eating all together, ever since Cassie death I haven't eaten at all, this was really beginning to put a toll on me. I can't live until I take their life, is the way my mind started to set my thoughts into place, he was a danger to me as long as he is still living on this fuckin earth, it's his life or mine. The more I thought the more my thoughts became over flowing from the cup I was holding, so I began to speak my thoughts out loud, as if I was losing my mind.

What am I so afraid of, I ain't afraid of shit, that's what!

But in reality, as long as he is alive, I will always be in fear of losing my life, as long as he around, you may say but why, I'm afraid about what he may later do or say, that ain't no way to live, in fear of a fuckin witness for the State of Ohio, what the fuck type of shit is that!

Before he went in the house, he checked all his surroundings, everything looked good so he moved forward into the house. He tried to adjust his eyes to the darkness, but whatever it was, is moving too fast for his eyes to catch up. The next best move for him were to turn around and get the hell out of there and witch he tried too, but as soon as he took a step back, he could feel the pistol on the small of his back.

Damn I just walked right into a trap, before I could turn around to see who had me at gun point, the figure that were moving in the dark had caught up to me fast, pow, pow, pow the shots started to ring out, I could instantly feel the pain shoot through my body.

Sharon:

As I reached over to pick up his phone off my passage seat after putting it down over and over again fighting with myself, the scent of him filled my nose which pushed her thoughts of him into overdrive, it only made me want him more and more each passing minute, as she began to look through his phone, she noticed he had a lot of missed calls and text messages from his friend Mike D.

Damn he blowing him the fuck up, what could be so damn important?

As soon as she opened the message, the first sentence set her heart to a blaze.

Lamar this is Mike D, I need you to hit me back ASAP Lil Rob over here talking about turning you in to the police for killing Cassie, he said he knew for a fact you were with her last night because he was the one who dropped her off at your house, then hours later she was found dead in the park. Bro call me none of this shit is making any sense, you got to tell me something!

I read it over and over again, and it only made my heartbeat go up to a hundred miles an hour, my head felt like it was under water, my stomach was ready to release everything that I ate this morning. O my God, my thoughts were all over the place, what am I going to do, damn could he had done this? What should I do? All I know is he needs my help!

She started the car and hit a u turn to race back by Lamar house to warn him and at the same time she started calling Lamar's dad over and over again to bring him up to date on what was going on. She felt that if anybody would know what to do it would be him.

Lamar:

Me and Lil Rob both hit the ground fighting for control of his gun, while the pain took over my body from the fall, bullets ricocheted all around me, I felt it was only a matter of time one would end up landing in my skull, ending the fight all at once. In one motion, I began to try to pull Lil Rob closer to me, hoping if I put Lil Rob in harm way of the gun fire that maybe it would crease but boy was I wrong, it only infuriated her and made her aim even harder to kill me.

Pow, pow, I am going to kill you motherfucker! She screamed at the top of her lung.

As we continued to fight I could hear the sirens coming in the distance, I knew I had to get out of there.

Come on Rob get the motherfucker!

At this point I could tell that I'm running out of time and I'm not gaining control so I did the only thing that was left for me to do, let go and go for my own gun.

The gun went off into Lil Rob stomach.

Noooo, Lil Rob mother screamed after she seen that he was hit.

His body went limp on top of me, as I rolled him over fighting to get to my feet, his mother rushed me and at this point, I were staring down the barrel of the gun, but I could not see my end so I just closed my eyes only to hear the click of the empty gun only inches from my face, I reached up and let off two shots in return, one catching her in the neck, the other landing right square in the middle of her chest, knocking her instantly to the ground, taking place of any words left for her to say, I closed in the space between us, keeping an eye contact with her before I released a rain of bullets into her corpse closing off any hope for an open casket, then I turn and ran into the woods, leaving them both behind me, not looking back not even for a second.

Detective Rainwater and Detective cooper responded to a shots fired call over the radio, they hit the sirens and began to run through every light that were in their path, trying their best to get to the scene as fast as they could.

What the hell is going on here said Detective Rainwater, with a strong look of anger in his face.

I don't know but this whole week has been real fuckin crazy, especially the killing of the little girl in the park, God she had so much life left to live and then for the boy and his mother to come in and make a statement about a 13-year-old boy doing all this, I mean literally has blown my mind, I didn't even think of this type of shit I was 13, damn if this is true, this kid is a fuckin monster that has to be stopped Rainwater, we got to get this kid off the streets! Said Detective Cooper.

The detectives pulled into the drive way and saw a body laid out in the drive way. The address clicked into Detective Rainwater head and he thought about the little boy and his mother, who just came downtown to make a statement down at the station earlier. Before the car could come to a complete stop Detective Rainwater was out of the car on his feet rushing to see what had happened, it was clear he was too late for the mother, the mother was already gone, she had experienced over kill, she had been shot so many times that the blood was pouring out of her from everywhere, the Detectives didn't know where to start if he wanted too, when he looked at her son, he could see there were still some movement, so he rushed to him to render aid on him to try to save the young man's life. As soon as Lil Rob seen the Detective, he tried hard to fight the words off the tip of his tongue, but blood began to pour out of his mouth uncontrollably.

Take it easy son help is on the way, don't try to talk, just stay with me, help will be here as soon as they can, Detective Cooper said as he tried his best to keep Lil Rob alive.

La, Lam, La, Lamar!

Hold on son, stay with me, Detective said but in fear that if they don't hurry soon, they were going to lose him.

La, Lam, Lamar, Lil Rob fought out.

Is this the one who did this to you son? Said Detective Rainwater trying to keep the boys eyes open.

Then out of nowhere Lil Rob started slipping away and before you know it, he was gone, with his eyes still open, staring into the sky, he had taken his last breath.

Got dammit Cooper! The Detective got up and punched at the air, kicked the garbage can on its side knocking it to the ground, spreading it all over the drive way.

Calm down Rainwater, this is now a crime scene!

We have to stop this little bastard from killing anybody else, Detective Rainwater said while pacing back and forth over Lil Rob's lifeless body.

We don't know for sure if he was the one who did this!

You got to be fucking kidding me! We know he did this shit! It was the boy last fuckin dying words and not to mention, these two just came down to the station earlier to make a statement against him, so that's motive! Then a couple hours later there fuckin dead! F'or Jesus Christ put two and two together, this is an open and shut case, you don't have to be a fucking rocket scientist Cooper!

Before Detective Cooper could say another word, Detective Rainwater stormed down the drive way and jumped into the car.

Where are you going Detective?

I'm going to bring that little bastard in for questioning!

But we don't have all of the facts just yet, we can't mess this up because how we feel about this, we shouldn't just rush into things, let's do this by the book.

It was almost as if he didn't pay him any attention.

I have to set eyes on this motherfucker and just maybe I could get him to tell me something, Detective Rainwater said to himself as he were pulling out the drive way.

Lamar:

As soon as I got home, my mind was all over the place. I had to get rid of the gun and the clothes, plus take a shower so I began to pour bleach all over me to try to kill the gun powder residue off my hands and anywhere else it might had landed on my body. If anything Mike D said was true, I know the police are going to be on their way here to get me pretty soon, never before have I ever been so messy. I couldn't turn my brain off, not even for a second. I was wrecking my brain wondering did I leave any evidence behind on the scene? Since I really didn't make it all the way in the house when this happen and we were outside, I started to worry about all kinds of things, damn what if somebody saw me? Now I would have to deal with another witness I would have to take care of down the line but I won't be able to take care of them if I don't know who they are! This was supposed to be the end of this situation, but as time goes on, shit is starting to get more and more fucked up for me, damn I need to talk to May-so, he would know what to do, he would show me what I'm supposed to do next! As I looked all over the house for my phone, I couldn't find it nowhere, shit where did I leave it, what if I dropped it by their house? Shit I was losing my mind, I ran to the house phone trying to remember his number as best as I can, and I knew I shouldn't call him on a home line but it felt like my head was under water, it felt like everything was coming to a dead end. Before I could get the number fully dialed, I could hear a strong knock at the door.

Boom, boom, boom, police!

The voice coming through the door were aggressive and strong, like if I don't answer in the next minute, they were going to kick the door down and come in and get me.

Boom, boom, boom, open up we know you're in there Lamar, we just want to ask you some questions! One of the officers said in an unbelievable tone.

When I looked out the window I could see two plain clothes cops standing by the door with their hands resting firmly on their guns. If I made any wrong moves, I knew in my heart they would gun me down the first chance they got, I checked into all the choices I had, which came out to be none, so I opened the door and as soon as I did they drew their guns.

Get your hands up or I'll shoot motherfucker!

I thought all you wanted to do was talk! I said as I watched their every move, I could feel all the blood draw from my face, this just might be the beginning to my end, now I know what May-so would say, I could hear him loud in clear in the back of my mind (Lamar say less).

Sharon:

As I'm flying through the traffic lights, trying to keep my composer in check, I started coming up on to the house. I could see the cop car lights flashing from a distance.

I'uck, fuck, fuck! I can't help but to scream out loud and take my frustration out on the steering wheel, like I were beating a high school drum. As I get closer, I could see them putting Lamar into the car and for the first time to me, he really looked his age, scared and more alone than ever. I didn't stop at the house, I have to go get him some help, I couldn't break down right now I know he needed me more than ever and if anybody will know what to do, his dad will.

Lamar:

As I sit in this room with the mirror staring back at me, it gives me a chance to work on my faces, I wanted to show no weakness, but the one I need to play the most were confused and scared, they might eat that up, that were the only card I had left to play, if not I might end up in prison for the rest of my life. The longer it took for them to enter the room; it gave me confidence they really didn't have nothing on me. At this point I'm going to choose to hide behind my age, which is at the moment my one and only defense, ain't no telling what Lil Rob told them.

Hello Lamar Wright, my name is Detective Rainwater and my partner name is Detective Cooper, we want to ask you some questions about some murders.

Somewhat! I said looking into his eyes trying to match mine like I been touched by the fear of God.

Yes, some murders! First let me ask you how do you know Cassie Humphrey? said Detective Rainwater.

She is a good friend of mine; I mean were a good friend of mines.

When were the last time you saw her and be honest because we will know if your lying we got evidence that we can cross reference with your story?

I don't know, maybe a few days ago.

With each question they began to get closer and closer to me until I was pinned between the two of them and more aggressive with their words. I could feel them breathing down my neck, they pulled out pictures of Cassie lifeless body to check for my reactions, they pushed me around and threaten my life and freedom over and over again, I never said a word. I could hear May-so words overpowering there in my mind, (Lamar say less) I told them I want to call my momma and started to cry uncontrollably thinking that would help me but it didn't. I knew what they were doing were illegal, they weren't even supposed to talk to me in the first place without an adult present. I'm a miner! I had to know just what they had on me, no matter how dangerous it was. It wasn't until they not only spoke about Lil Rob and his mom but they also mention Money Mo as well, then I realize shit was getting real from all angles. They had my attention, I sat up in my seat, wipe my face and said those magic words I should of spoke hours ago, that would have put all this bullshit to rest.

I want to talk to a lawyer!

I watched as their face lost its color, but even then, there was still an attempt to ignore my request and then out of nowhere the door flies open and my father and unidentified white man step into the room demanding their attention.

Stop this! Enough of this! You guys should be ashamed of yourself, talking to my client without an adult or an attorney present. I could have your necks for this said the attorney, pointing his finger at the Detectives in anger.

The Detectives backed into a corner like they had broken momma's rules and quickly been put on punishment.

I was just asking him a couple of questions, no harm done said Detective Rainwater. Release him this instant!

He is not under arrest he could have left any time he wanted too, we were just asking questions, said Detective Cooper.

Detective Rainwater tapped him on his side, almost to say in so many words, just let him go.

But it was too late, the words of Detective Cooper, put a fire under the attorney feet, I could see the rage build up in his eyes.

You got to be fuckin kidding me! You have no evidence against my client, yet you have him here hand cuffed to a chair saying he's been free to go the whole time! He's a miner there is no adult present showing him pictures of the murder victims, with that alone is enough to kiss both of you guys fuckin careers goodbye! Now fuckin release him out of them cuffs and believe me, you will not be hearing the last of this, as a matter of fact don't be surprised if we don't file a lawsuit against your whole department for this!

Detective Rainwater released me and took a step back to get out my way, we locked eyes for a second and I could see the determination to get me in his eyes at that moment I knew this would not be the last time we see each other.

All the whole ride home my dad was on my back, like he been there from day one and he never left, I just couldn't let it go, I had to speak my mind.

Dad what's up with you?

What you mean! What's up with me? What the hell up with you? You got yourself caught up in some shit son, what if you didn't get me that money? I would not have been able to get you a lawyer!

Thank you! But the truth is, I didn't ask you to do none of that shit! I got this all under control, they ain't got nothing on me!

Nothing on you like you didn't do it? Or nothing like they didn't find no evidence.

I didn't answer, I just looked out the window with a blank expression on my face, I just don't know if I could trust him with the truth, but I have to say something, I could just leave the conversation up in the air, the way I really wanted to keep it.

Dad, naw I didn't do it and you know that I would tell you what's going on, you know that.

He held a face of disbelief and struggled with his words as if he didn't know what to say next, so he started beating around the brush for what he really wanted. I just listened.

Son I care about you, I love you, I don't know what I would do if something were to happen to you, and I ain't going to lie, this shit really kind of scares me because the police have to have something to come talk to you in the first place. Ow listen to me I know you got some money put up, you need to let me know where you keep it, not to hold it or nothing but just in case you need me again I could get to it for you.

Once again I didn't answer and over the next couple of weeks, that same question would come up in our conversations over and over again. No matter if he is my dad or not I knew I couldn't give up that type of information but I had to tell him something or he was never going to give it up, so I told him that my mom holds my money so he would put this conversation to rest and everything was all good for a while. With everything going on, I Mike D and Lil Will on to the hustle and stayed completely out the way because I knew the police would be watching. While I were on the block with a couple of my guys just chilling because it was a beautiful day outside, watching the Lil honey's go past, I get a phone call from my dad, talking about he needed to see me and that he couldn't talk over the phone so damn it must be important. I agreed to meet up with him. When we got off the phone I begin to get in my own head a little bit, which was placing me on the edge. I began to wonder just what was so important, not long after we got off the phone, he pulled up waving trying to get my attention as he pulled up to the curve. As soon as he parked, he jumped out the car and motioned with his hands for me to come to him, now as I came to him, he motioned for me to get in the driver sit as he got in the back seat directly behind me, he had some white woman with him riding in the front sit. I asked who she was and he told me it was some woman he just started dating. All this was beginning to feel weird to me. As we began to ride, he introduced us, while he was talking, I took a look into his eyes through the rearview mirror to get a feel on the reason of him coming. The look, was a look I seen before but only in a junkie's eyes, damn was he high? Hell naw! I'm tripping.

Dad what's going on, when you called me it seems like you had something real important to tell me.

I do have something to tell you but I really want to get you and your mom in the same room so we all can sit down and talk all at once and do you got your gun on you? If so let me see it.

Why do you need to talk to my mom? And why do you need to see my gun? What's going on with you? What are you worried about? Believe me pop you good with me, I said looking back at him through the rearview mirror.

He got irritated with me!

Boy let me see your damn gun! It's shit going on and we need to have each other backs, so just give it to me, I'll explain ever hing later.

I reached in the small of my back and handed my dad my Glock 17 and immediately after I did it, I felt out of place, Mayso always told me to never give anyone my gun and take a ride with no direction. I had giving my dad the bottle and now he was babysitting my cup. As soon as he got my gun it was a look in his eyes I had never seen before and I couldn't put my hand on what it was but it made me feel real uncomfortable, it's not fear, not worry, it seems like he was deep in thought, about what? I don't know, but I have to pick his brain a little bit.

Dad where are we going?

I told you we have to meet up with your mom, we all might be in danger, he said looking off to out the window.

Dad my momma isn't home yet.

Before I could finish what I were about to say, I now know where I recognize that look, it was a look full of hunger and greed, it was a look I share every morning in the mirror. It made me think for the first time. Damn would he try to rob me? Naw that's my family, I'm his son! Damn that would be a new one for me but where I'm from not unheard of. The more I drove the more thoughts filled my mind. Damn I could be tripping, I tried to laugh my thoughts off but I just couldn't hide my concern on my face.

Are you ok baby, said the white lady who name I never got. Yes, I'm fine.

I just hoped I was wrong, but if I'm not, I could have just given away my last chance in the fight. As I pulled into the apartment complex of what he thought were my mom's house. I did one more look in the rearview and then one more look to the passage side to look in the face of the unknown white lady as I pulled into the closest parking spot I could, a shot rang out, I reach for the door so I could get out of the car, I needed to see where the shots were coming from, but before I could get out the car, two more shots sounded off in my ear and at the same time I could feel an unbearable pain enter into my back, I had been shot and it wasn't clear on where the shots was coming from until I was laying on my back bleeding out of control outside the car and my dad were standing over me with my gun pointed directly at my head.

Come on come on we got to go! The lady said.

Shut up Robin! He said never taking his eyes off of me. Dad what are you doing? Why are you doing this?

I fuckin hate you! If your momma wasn't a virgin, I would've never claimed you! Now I need that money so where is it before I shoot you in the face!

Is this what this is about, money?

I could feel my body getting weaker and weaker with each and every passing minute, was this it? Was this the end for me? Was all I could think about as I stared down the other side of the barrel.

Ok fuck it then, you ain't got to tell me, I'll follow your momma home after your funeral!

Then another shot rang out coming within inches of my head, I back paddle as much and as fast as I could to try to get away but the pain from the shots would not let me move any farther.

Where the fuck is the money and put some speed on it, I'm not going to miss the next shot mafucka! He said as he were walking me down to finish me off.

Before I could open my mouth I could see the police bending the corner but will they make it in time before he finished the job, my eyes began to get heavy and before I knew it I was out, the next time I open my eyes I were laying on the doctors table and the doctors and nurses are pumping on my chest, tube were going down my throat, I could feel the pain but the pain from my heart over powered the shots I just took.

Hurry! Hurry! We are losing him we need to get him to the ER!

My soul had been crushed from my dad's betrayal mentally I died on that table. I lost all taste for love. My own father didn't want to spare my life, instead he set me up to rob me, then kill me!

He even planned my funeral in his head, I left $50,000 in my momma house to throw the robbers off of my trail, in their mind, that was a lot of money, I knew they would have thought they had taken everything I had, that was something I learned from Money Mo. All I know now is I need to get out of this hospital before the police come by asking questions but I can't move and my eyes are so heavy, I did the only thing I could do which is lay there and rest. When I open my eyes from resting, the detectives were standing over me, questioning the nurses about my condition.

Who did this to you? Was the first question they asked before I could get my eyes all the way open.

As they search my face for answers, I search my thoughts for what's next, while they are talking to me, the voices in my mind is over powering there every word. A part of me had stepped outside my body and I was no longer in the room.

Mr. Wright you have to tell us something or we won't be able to help you, the person is still out there, now who knows if they are going to try and come get you again, they could kill you the next time, does what happen today have anything to do with what we questioned you about?

Maybe they are trying to get a little revenge on you for what you did!

Without saying one word, tears started running down my face and all I could do is look in the direction of the window, I got nothing to say and there is nothing they could do or say to change that. For the next couple of days', the detectives kept on coming but nothing changed, I had nothing for them, my mom was there the whole time, she never left my side, I wanted to tell her what happen but I couldn't. I knew things would only get worse, if she truly knew what happen she would be the first person to involve the police, she is nothing like me, she would want to see him under the jail and that wouldn't be enough for me because I just want to see him dead. Once I left the hospital, I didn't want to go home, I only wanted to go to the one place I knew I would be safe, where no one would look for me, my Grandma Vickie house, she, other than May-so is the only one I could trust, at this point my head is all screwed up and my grandma Vickie would know what I should do. When I walked into the house I was greeted by nothing else but love, we sat on the back porch and talked about everything. Sometimes during our conversation, I would break down and cry. My heart was hurting in so many ways. We talked about what we think I should do and that were ok but it was one thing my grandma Vickie said that stood out to me the most, never gamble your life, especially when it comes to love, love will blind you every time.

Those same words played in my mind over and over again. Burning a hole in my brain, I had to get focused, instead of rushing into things I decided to just lay low and I did just that. Five years had gone by and no one from the old hood had seen me, I disappeared into thin air over night, my grandmother put me in a nice Lil spot out the way, I had got my health all the way back together, she helped me get my strength back together, those shots had done a lot of damage to my body, the Detectives didn't let up, they kept showing up at my mother house, it kind of feels like I'm on the run, leaving made me look even more guilty but I had to leave to clear my head. Now it was time to go back and face everything I just couldn't run forever. I knew deep down in my heart I couldn't stay here forever, the first person I planned on seeing my first day back was my boy Mike D, it's been five years and I wondered just how life had been treating him, I tried to go to his house but him and his brother had moved after his grandmother passed. The word is, she had been battling cancer for some time now, I guess it got really bad after I left. I got ahold of Mike D number from a couple of cats that use to hang down by the store. I called a couple of times but he never answered after a couple of days I guess he checked his calls and hit me back. He told me he came across my number checking to see if he missed any licks, and that's another thing, the streets can talk and they been saying that since I haven't been around Mike D and Lil Will been running the show in the streets. While Mike D did get his money up, it was real clear that Lil Will was the one really in charge. I was surprised to hear all the moves that been made. They told me how they got their start, they told me when I had brought the bag of drugs and money to their house, Lil Will took some of the weed and money and never looked back after that day. I wasn't tripping because a lot of the money were for them in the first place, I just didn't expect a lot of shit to go wrong the way it did and it made things hard for me to make it back to them to collect what was mines. When Mike D came to see me much of what we talked about were the good old days. He made it seem like it was forever ago the last time we seen each other. But then out of nowhere I saw a deep seriousness come across his face.

Man Lamar, I got some shit to tell you, I almost let slip my mind!

I instantly thought he were start bullshitting me when it came to the money he owes me and that was something I wasn't willing to forgive.

What's this about my money you owe me? Because if it is I hope your next words is going to be a got you, I ain't up for no bullshit.

Mike D stared into my eyes surprised that I would even say such a thing.

What bro, man look I got your money and some! You ain't never got to worry about me playing you, especially about no money I love you bro!

Ok cool what's up then bro, what's good?

Mike D walked in real close and dropped his tone to a whisper, keeping our conversation in private even dough we were by ourselves, I mean no one was around, he made it seem like we were in a room full of people.

Bro word around town is this nigga name Skillz been laying on you, waiting for you to slip. What you mean?

He been telling mafucka's around town that you had something to do with some guy named Money Mo getting killed.

What! Man nigga please! Skep Dollar went to prison for that body! I was cool with Money Mo he was like a mentor to me in the hustle game but I ain't have shit to do with that shit! I was just a Lil nigga when he died. People always running they mouth about shit they think happen, putting bullshit out in the air for another mafucka to smell it!

No! no! no! he telling mafucka's he saw you driving Money Mo car that morning he got killed, he said it was real early and you were going into the house with some big ass black garbage bags and might I add, he said Money Mo was worth a couple of million.

And you believe this bullshit? I asked with playful eyes.

Hell null, I told him he must got the wrong person in mind because you ain't got no money, especially no millions I know you would of rode off into the sunset by now!

We both laughed at what Mike D had said, but in truth I knew this shit meant more trouble coming my way, I thought I got away clean but I guess I didn't and now I got to go see about Skillz.

Bro you got to show me who he is, I don't want someone around me and I don't even know who he is and he got beef with me, shit that's just like giving your life away.

No bro it ain't going to come to that, we gone get ahead on that, don't worry, Mike D said as he patted me on my back.

And get ahead of it is what we tried to do, for weeks and weeks all we would do is slide, hide and move, looking for Skillz, stalking his chill spots, robbing all the blocks he been known to hustle on, never speaking a name but still sending the message, he would know it was me, he just woke up a sleeping bear and poked it with nonsense. Once he spoke openly about me out personally, everything that will happen next is going to be real personal as well. We did a little more moving around looking for him but Skillz still didn't show his face. In my mind, he ran because he knows that I'm looking for him or he is truly a man of patience when it comes to war. Neither one of those options bother me, not knowing who he is or how he looks is what bothers me the most. After we stopped robbing Skillz peoples and looking for him all together. It was back to getting money, we started breaking down everything we took in the robbers and started grinding it all out. Just waiting to see if he would eventually pop up, lately my days has been bright, I been drinking and eating BBQ, chilling heavy after everything through I just been really trying to relax, the trap was jumping out of control, the licks were running in and out, so many people, it got to the point that we didn't even lock the door anymore. For some reason lately I been feeling out of place, sometimes it could only seem like shit is going good right before shit end up going bad, I could feel it because we been having our guard down like crazy. Me, Mike D, and Lil Will was talking about picking back up our search for Skillz we couldn't just let this rest, it's been a while I know he has hit the surface by now. I talked Lil Will into going to the store for us to get some more drank and cigars, we had a couple of girls over I wanted to get them loaded and hopefully I could get lucky and release some of this pressure I been holding on too for the last couple of weeks. As Lil Will was going out the door two guys pushed pass him inti the house. One of the guys I knew from 1300 block but the other guy I never seen before, the one I knew from 1300 block, I didn't even know his name but he was a real common face around the area, we never did business before, it's not even clear to me how he would even know where I live, but then again this is a word of mouth hustle, everybody buys weed from us so it ain't no secret where people could find us. What bother me was the look in the other guy's eyes that made me feel unsettled, I tried to find a reason for this feeling but I couldn't, damn I just couldn't.

Hey what's up my guy, how can I help you? I said watching there every movement.

What's up Lamar bro I just came through to grab a Lil something to smoke before I go in the house and watch the Lakers game tonight, I'm ready to call it a day I had a long day at work, the guy from 1300 block said but making sure he never connected in eye contact.

I didn't take my eyes off the guy with the crazy eyes, as he got all the way in my house he locked the door behind him, I looked around to see where Mike D were and that's when I noticed that he was in the other room with his Lil lady friend, it was just me and the girl who came to see me Jazz and these two dudes that gave me a really bad vive in my gut. My gun was on the table and I didn't know if I should go for it or keep it cool, after all I could be just over reacting or really fuckin slipping!

Yea bro I got you, and listen this shit I got, you can't smoke all at once unless you really ready to call it a day because this shit will definitely put you straight to sleep.

Come on now, this B Luck you talking too, I smoke like a chimney baby! Ain't to much can put my ass to sleep!

As he came closer to overlook what I had, the other guy stayed in the corner with his arm's folded not saying a word or changing the look on his face he started with. I could hear Mike D coming from the back room, so I made sure I didn't move to fast, but I had to make a move for my gun without causing a scene. I didn't want them to feel like I would rob them but I didn't want to be the one getting robbed either! I made up a couple of bags for B Luck and right as I was about to hand it to him, Mike D walked into the room.

Skillz! What are you doing here bro?

As soon as I heard the name, my heart went directly into my stomach. I moved even faster to my gun but Skillz stopped me in my tracks when he pulled out two twin Glock's from under his shirt, damn I had been caught off guard and now once again I'm staring down the barrel of this gun, just waiting on it to click or the quick flash of light to speak, which ever one that comes lfst!

Hey! Hey! Hey! Heyyyyy now! You reach for that gun Lamar and I promise you I'm gone shoot you right in your fuckin face! Skillz said as he slid across the room like he was wearing skates. My first thought was to fight, but if I made the wrong move I knew shit could get really messy, I have to put my mind to work before it ended up being too late. When I look to the left I could see Jazz crying begging for them to let her go, shaking out of control. When I look to the right B Luck had start beating Mike D repeatedly over the head with his gun, trying to get him to lay on the floor, for a moment I was mute from all sound, what actually snapped me back on point was the gun smashing against my head.

Smack! Smack! Skillz hit me to get my attention.

You hear me mafucka! Where that shit at before I kill you?

I played dumb hoping it would buy me some time to think. Bro what shit? I said as if I didn't know.

Mafucka you know what shit I'm talking about! O you think I'm playing?

The look in his eyes told me In so many words that playing around with him would be the wrong thing to do, he gave me a vibe like he itching to kill something, I don't know what I'm going to do but I got to do something!

O so you want to act stupid huh, like I didn't see you that morning Money Mo got killed carrying them bags. At first I didn't think nothing of it when I saw you until he popped up on the news and the car I seen you driving end up set on fire in front of Money Mo right hand man house.

Skillz what the fuck is you talking about? They caught the guy that did that shit to him!

Yeah they caught him, but he could not of did that shit alone, when they caught him he didn't even have a car, how did he kill Money Mo momma and daughter, then go to Money Mo house and kill him and his wife with no car? The bus! A cab! Lol Naw what I think is you was driving and you got greedy and ended up leaving homeboy. He gets caught so you can keep all the money to yourself, he said.

Skillz man you crazy! I don't have no money! if I had the type of money that Money Mo had I would not still be grinding out here still in the streets, I would have moved my family out of here already!

Tell me anything huh, I should just kill you right now and just say fuck this money! He said with the hate in his eyes.

As I'm trying to get the blood out of my eyes, he's pointing the gun at my head, he looks as if he is moving in closer for the kill, I closed my eyes preparing for the worse.

Skillz! Skillz! Come on bro, we can't kill them, we need to get our hands on that money! We ain't come here to caught a body for nothing, come on man don't kill him man!

B Luck plead with Skillz to spare my life, which gave me some more time to figure something out neither one of us were talking and I could see they were getting madder and madder by the minute, they got us all face down and tied up on the floor, I know they been here for a while so it's clear they can't find nothing, I got to make a move before it's too late.

Skillz! B Luck! A come here man! Let me holla at you, I said as I tried to pick myself up off the floor.

They rushed back into the room like 'vicious animals looking for their next spot to feed. What's up motherfucker, you got something to tell us?

I could show you where the money is but you got to untie me, let everybody go and I'll take you!

O you think this shit is a game huh, you think you can just place your demands and act as if you have a choice in this bitch! But to give up the bag or be in a bag by the time I leave is the only choice you truly have!

Pow! Pow!

He shot pass my head, almost hitting me in the face.

What the fuck bro, I said trying to get away from him.

My ears had begun to ring out of control, Skillz then started beating me over the head to the point I started losing consciousness.

Get the fuck up right now, ok you know what!

Skillz walked straight behind the girl Mike D was with and put the gun to her head.

Fuck the games he said, as he pulled the trigger, the bullet entered the back of her head and exited out the front spreading her brains all over the wall and on the face of Mike D who was standing next to her. She was dead before she even hit the ground, damn!

Now keep acting like you don't know what's going on, I'm gone kill everybody around you, and save your ass for last! Skillz said with the hunger for more blood in his eyes.

Come on man I'll take you to the money, just don't kill nobody else!

He untied me and walked me to the bedroom in the back, I never stopped talking and I kept my eyes on him the whole time, I took him to the closet, I have a little dummy pack set up there and this just might be my only way out. When we got to the closet I tried to open the door but Skillz ran me to the wall.

Listen to me motherfucker! If you try anything I'm not going to hesitate to fuckin kill you, you see what I just did to that bitch! You could think I'm playing if you want to.

He forced the gun into my mouth and down my throat causing me to choke, I started to fight back as much as I could without forcing him into pulling the trigger.

I been watching you for years, and you pretty smart; you got that money put up somewhere good and you think you about to give me some dummy pack and we gone run off, no! no! Noooo!

That's not how this is going to work, depending on how good the dummy bag is, gone depend on if I'm going to let your friends live or not. Then I'm going to take you with me and torture you every day until you show me where the real bag is at! Now come on and get that shit! Come on! He said as he pushed me toward the closet. He backed up, giving me a little space but not too much, he was watching my every move, but I have to try him, right next to the bag of money is a small .380 locked and loaded, ready to go! But I also know he is on me tight, if I go for the gun, he just might see me and gun me down, so I got to throw him off, I reached down and open the bag then stepped back.

Here take this shit Skillz! It's not worth my life!

He smacked me right up side my head with the butt of the gun. Get that shit, you think I'm gone let you get behind me! You think I'm stupid motherfucker?

He pushed me down into the closet to grab the bag for him, just how I wanted it, to my advantage, after I caught my balance, I reached for the gun with one hand and the dummy bag with the other hand. I placed the bag in front of the gun to hide it from his view. As soon as he seen the money over flowing out of the top of the bag. He lowered the gun and with the other hand, reached for the bag, then that's when all hell broke loose, I tossed the bag up in the air then I let off three shots landing all, one in his face and two in his chest, through all of that he was still able to stumble back and get off a shot, which almost hit me by inches but landed into the wall instead. I went to shoot a couple more shots to finish the job but the gun jam! So I ran into the bathroom so I would be shielded from any more gun fire that might be coming my way. As soon as I got the gun unjammed I went back into the room within seconds I seen someone enter into the room, with no hesitation and without looking, I shot and backed back into the bathroom.

When I heard the screams, I looked back out the door way, I realized the one who ran into the room was Jazz! I had shot her in the leg and she was bleeding like crazy. The blood was pouring out of her leg like a public water fountain, as I ran past her looking for Skillz and B Luck, Jazz pulled for me pleading for me not to leave her. I ran out into the hallway, Skillz was laid face down in the stairwell in a pool of blood, Mike D had left me, he was nowhere to be found, I ran back into the house and looked out the window, I seen B Luck limping like he had been shot, I started firing shots out the window, crowds of people started running in every direction so it became hard to tell if I hit B Luck or not! As I pull my head back into the window I could hear the cops coming from a distance, I realize that I had to get rid of all the weed we had stashed in the house, so I ran and opened everything up and started throwing it out the window, I hid the guns and tried my best to get Jazz outside the apartment, but as soon as I opened the door the police were right on the other side. They rushed in and threw me on the ground, the ambulance rushed to Jazz and tried to stop the bleeding. When they sat me up and I looked around, all I could see is one big mess. I got a dead girl in my living room, a dead guy is face down in my stairwell, the Jazz was shot and I got caught trying to drag her out of the house and to make things worse, they are doing test on my hands looking for gun residue, she is not even conscious, while the ambulance is working on her all she keeps saying is:

What you do Lamar? Lamar what did you do?

Damn it looks like I'm in some deep shit, all by myself! Mike D ran off so it's my story is the only story that will be told, I didn't get the chance to get rid of all the pounds of weed. I don't think I'm gone get away with this one. I know I'm going to have to do some time in prison for this. I got to fight this that's all I know. I could get life from the bodies alone. They picked me up and walked me down to the car, the whole time I could feel my legs getting weaker and weaker with each step. They passed the county jail, so I knew right then, this was going to be a long night. I had no one to call, to get me out of this and that hurt me bad, I knew those Detectives was going to want a part of me even dough time had passed. I know they hadn't forgot shit how could they!

Hey now, look who we got here! Where the hell have you been Mr. Wright? We haven't seen you in a while!

How are you Detective?

I knew he was gone pop back up murders have to feed, and killing people is just how they do it! Said Detective Rainwater.

No Detective this is real life, not the fuckin movies, I said in a joking way but still letting my anger shine through.

Yeah! Yeah! Yeah! Boy I'm so glad that you fuckin know the difference between fake and real life! We finally got something that will stick to your ass like glue, from what I hear there was bodies all over the place and they caught you with a smoking gun, your ass is done if you ask me!

Detective no! no! no! I'm the victim here! They came in the house to rob me!

And what? You killed him and the girl, plus shot the other guy up really bad, yea we know the other guy, that got away from your wrath you unleashed! Detective Cooper said while shaking his head.

The wrath I unleashed! What are you talking about? I said with the most confused look on my face.

Come on now! Let's not do that now, you know what we talking about, o and Lamar your boy B Luck wrote a statement you and he told us everything that happen from the beginning to the end, as a matter of fact I don't think he left out one little detail!

I couldn't help it, I laughed him off, but in my mind, I was lost in thought. I can't believe that he came to rob me and now he's working with the police. Damn he wrote a statement on me, and he told everything that happen but in reverse! Everything they done to me, he said I did to him and yes, he is willing to testify, he said that Mike D killed Skillz and I killed the girl and shot him as he were trying to get away. As of right now Mike D is on the run so I'm fucked until they get his side of the story. I said nothing, but I ain't gone lie, I wonder how

Mike D are going to take the news when he finds out that he was the one who killed Skillz and he has an eye witness, knowing he didn't do nothing at all! I feel it's not my place to set the record straight and I'm sorry to say, now that they took that body off of me I could prove I wasn't the one who killed the girl, because of Jazz, she got shot but she can let the truth be known as well, I mean shit, she has too, besides Mike D and B Luck, she is the only other person that lived. Damn this shit is messy, I told them I wanted a lawyer and the interview stopped and when it did, the Detectives placed me under arrest and took me to a cell and shut the door. Damn when that door slam, it put a weight on my soul, the lights are on when the lights is off, just tinted, I can't sleep, I just laid there, facing the wall, living second by second into my thoughts after each and every thought, I put in there, damn what am I going to do now? I think about all I been through and all the things that I wish I could change, it felt like forever for the morning to come. I rushed it, I beg for the morning to come I have to make some calls, I have to figure something out! Before I knew it the door popped open and the guard was calling breakfast, I stepped out of the cell, and seen all walks of life around me, from bums who slept on the streets, to drug addicts got caught chasing a fix to somebody who could have got pulled in from a major drug bust to one caught on a murder rap like me, you don't know who you dealing with from one conversation to the next. The stress and pain filled the air in the whole room. This is for sure a place I have to watch myself, watch who is watching me, and speaking of watching me, it's been this cat named Low, every time I turn around, this guy is either just around me in the area or butting into my conversations! It's almost like he trying to read me or something, he was interested in me more than normal. So I put up my guard quick, questioning his every move, fake name throwing and all, after a week the truth came out. He told me that Skep Dollar is telling everyone he comes across that some nigga named Lamar Wright set him up and got him all his time in the joint. I picked him for more and more information without making him suspicious. He told that the dude Lamar had money on his head!

So how much money on his head? Shit I might have to get that myself and how did the dude Lamar actually get him the time or did he even say?

Yeah! You know what he said.

If I fuckin knew what he said I would not have fuckin asked you! I said.

Damn hold on bro, you acting like you mad, or like you know the dude or something! Fuck you talking about?

If you know this mafucka or if you are that mafucka let it be known, that's what I'm talking about! Low said as he approached me.

I smacked him, ready to put this shit in its place before it got out of hand.

What the fuck you talking about, you acting like you want some work! I said ready to swing on him again.

He backed down and began to stay in his place, in this place you have to show your strength, you can't have a weak moment. People will take advantage of that. I learned a lot over these last couple of days, Skep Dollar got me painted out to be a rat going around in the jail and possibly the whole prison where ever he is at! Yeah I set the nigga up, but that was only to take the fall. I ain't never got on no stand against nobody, I never have and I never will, all I know is that I'm gone have to put a stop to all this, cause one thing I ain't never been is no rat! I just play the game how it was taught to me and live by the code of the streets one that can't be broken. After a couple more days and a few hundred calls later, I made bond, yea one of the only people who truly loves me, I had nobody else to turn too, I knew she would be there, and she came, but I have to tell you, she was not happy!

Hi grandma,

Don't fuckin hi grandma me! Get your ass in this car, what the fuck are you doing? She asked with anger pouring through her eyes.

What you mean?

What the hell you mean! What you don't know? You been in the streets all this time and no one told you about the squeeze huh? Is that what it is! You can't take no pressure? So you on my line, blowing my phone down for me to come get you! And you still up to the same old shit!

When will enough be enough? You ain't gone learn until they kill you or they put you in jail for the rest of your life! You got money what else could you want? Damn why can't you just stay the fuck out of trouble?

No grandma, it's not like that, I just didn't have no one else to call!

Then sit the fuck still, you think I don't know what's going on with you while you in the streets, I'm always watching your back, putting in work behind the scenes, but look as soon as you feel a Lil pressure then you blow!

Blowing down the phone, ok I got it and I won't do that no

more, I'll make sure I stay patient, but I ain't say nothing! I don't crack under pressure I just didn't want to stay in there.

Yeah, I understand that! But now they might want to watch me, knock me down, trace our finances, just trying to get to you! That was a lot of money I posted for your bond!

I laughed stuck in my thoughts, but she was right, I wasn't thinking about all that. I can't get her caught up in this, not only was she all I have but she is my life line through everything. Grandma Vickie stayed on her toes, I get a lot of how I move from her, speaking of moves I got to slide across town and holla at Jazz, I caught the word while I was locked up that she is only 17, so her momma trying to make her testify and I don't mean on my behave either, if this happen, shit could get really bad for me. As soon as I got to my grandma's house I asked can I use her car so I could get ahead of this. I told her what was going on and that I needed to go see her. When she came out the house, she hugged and kissed me, she seemed really happy to see me, I asked her how she had been healing up, she told me about all the problems she been coming across as we smoked joint after joint out in the car, we talked about everything but the case as a matter of fact, she tried to stay off the topic altogether, until I pushed the issue.

Jazz what's good? I need you to be real with me baby!

Her eyes showed signs of worry, but she played it off like everything was fine.

Everything good! Why do you keep asking me that, Lamar what's all this really about? I ask Jazz, because the word around town is you planning on testifying on me!

That's what my momma want me to do, but I don't know!

Jazz what is there not to know? If it wasn't for me, we all would be dead! They were going to kill us all! You know that don't you?

I don't want to testify! It's my momma, she gone make me testify! Jazz what the fuck is wrong with you, I can't go to jail!

I reached into my waist band and grabbed my .40 caliber and sat it down on the arm rest of the car. As soon as Jazz seen the gun, she began to stumble over every word, she spoke next.

I! I! I! don't want you locked up Lamar I love, love you!

As she backed into the comer, my mind told me to kill her, don't allow her to get on the stand, but my heart held me back, me and Jazz had been friends since we were kids, so instead of killing her, I paid her off not to come to court. Even then, I knew my heart would get me in trouble, I knew I should have followed my intuition and I didn't, I just hoped that it would not come back to haunt me, afier I left Jazz a lot of shit went downhill and two days later I got rearrested for murder and possession of marijuana over the exceeded bolt. From this very moment I have a fight on my hands, as soon as they booked me in, I found out Jazz was there number one person to testify. A mafuckin star witness for the prosecution! Each court date was like 15 months away each time, I wasn't mad anymore, it gave me enough time to try to build my knowledge in the law and for the first time in my life, work on my relationship with the lord, I prayed more than I ever prayed in my life and I hope it works, I made promises and one of them was if you get me out of this, I'll never live this type of life again, I'll never kill again for no reason, I knew that promise was going to get me in trouble. Now it's time to see if my prayers worked because my day in court has come.

State of Ohio vs Lamar Wright.

We are looking to put in a plea today Mr. Wright, sir please stand and address the court please. I did exactly what I were told and put in my plea of not guilty.

The judge stared right through me, looking down on me as if I was nothing, I just knew in my heart that if they do find me guilty, I might not ever see day light again, as the trial went on they brought out witness after witness, people I never seen before, that had nothing to do with the case, up on the stand, speaking on what they think happen, painting a picture of me to ugly to let the world see but yet the jury has a front row seat, every word I say is equally important to every word that I don't. the sweat was pouring down my face, shit what the hell is next? Then the bailiff called in the next witness.

The State of Ohio calls Brain Boyd, to the stand. Brain Boyd come to the front please. I'm here! I'm here!

I saw the name on the list and never could connect the name to anybody I know until he walked into the court room, now I know that Brian Boyd is also known as B Luck, when he came in, he had his head held up high, you can see he was truly happy in his position, and then he got on the stand and all hell broke loose.

Brain Boyd do you swear to tell the truth, and nothing but the truth, so help you God? I do! he said while he was standing in front of the court.

After he said I do, nothing else made sense, he began to lose himself in his stories, going beyond the questions even going as far as crying for more attention and it was working because he has their attention, I look over to my lawyer, lean over and asked him to stop this, the whole time he's sitting back doing nothing, I couldn't take it anymore, I had to say something.

Your honor!

The whole courtroom came to a pause to give me the floor, my lawyer tried to pull me down as if he wanted me to stop.

Yes, Mr. Wright go ahead!

I would like to put in an oral motion to the court to become the lead counsel on my case.

My lawyer jumped to his feet, trying to force his way into the conversation, which was crazy, this was the most he has done all day.

Your honor can we move for recess so me and my client can talk!

There is no need your honor for a recess! I wish to be in full control of this case seating my attorney as the assistant counsel.

The judge spoke with a smirk on his face as if he had me right where he wanted me. And you are acting knowingly and intelligently on your decision to be lead counsel? Yes, your honor!

Ok then, Mr. Wright, proceed.

And proceed is what I did, first I attacked the evidence, I made B Luck talk about the guns, which person had what, then I refer back to the interview statement that he made with the officers, to show how his story has changed over a hundred times. Then I went back and attacked his story as a whole. He stumbled over his every word. Lost his eye contact after every question I asked, the tables had turned, the ball was now in my court, I had poked big holes into his credibility with the jury, now it was time to drop the big bomb on him.

Mr. Boyd when you came into this courtroom you had everyone thinking you were the victim! Mr. Wright! The Judge said trying to get my attention but I had to get it out.

That everyone was getting killed around you and you escaped, barely with your life, is that right? Mr. Wright! You are out of line!

But the truth is, you came to rob us and almost got yourself killed in the process police ass nigga, it was self-defense!

Mr. Wright stop this at once! You are not supposed to ask leading questions or badger the witness! The judge said with anger pouring out his eyes.

Your right your honor! I move to strike what I just said from the record!

The jury watched in surprise as I acted as if I had been a lawyer my whole life, what's sad is they thought I would fail the moment I stood up.

Your honor! I'm done testifying, I don't have nothing left to say, B Luck said as he dropped his head in front of the jury.

No! no! no! don't stop yet Mr. Boyd! We just now getting to the good part! O yeah and what part is that? said B Luck.

Let's talk about the address that all this happen at! I said to him as I moved in closer.

The closer I got, the more B Luck began to stumble over each and every word he spoke. You could tell that his nerves were starting to get the best of him, he didn't want to answer the question I just asked.

Ok! How about I help you out Mr. Boyd and tell the court myself, who house it was, to speed up the process a little, it was!

Mr. Wright! You cannot speak for the witness! The judge said, as I could tell he were truly starting to lose patience with me by the minute.

I just kept going, even dough the judge kept jumping in the conversation trying his best to stop me the best he could, I just ignored him, I pushed even harder.

Ok! Your right your honor, I can't speak for the witness, but can the witness talk to the jury? Can we talk about the address?

There is nothing to talk about when it comes to the address, let's just talk about how you robbed and shot those innocent people! Said B Luck trying to change the subject to get the light off of him that was shining so bright.

While B Luck was talking, Mike D walked into the court. As soon as he seen him, his body showed signs of wanting to run right out of the courtroom, everybody turned and stared.

Your honor, that was my apartment! That was my address where all this happen, Mike D said as he continued to walk towards the front.

Excuse me! But who are you said the Judge, looking for someone to give him some answers. I'm Michael Denton sir, I mean your honor!

Detective rainwater spoke, your honor Michael Denton was another suspect we have been looking for involved in this case as well.

Ok! Detain him!

And just like that the tables had turned once again, at that very moment Mike D had turned himself into the court but willing to speak on my behalf. I pushed for the court to let him testify to what happen on that day, the judge agreed, each and every jury watched him with close eyes as he told our story. He had to be telling the truth or a crazy man to come in here in the first place, but when he spoke all the evidence matched his story and the prosecutor couldn't even attack it, you could tell he was speaking from the heart, once everything was done, then came the verdict.

It took them hours to come back with the decision, I was scared because after everything I didn't know how all this was going to turn out.

The judge spoke:

The jury has made their decision, so we are ready to proceed.

Everyone stood up as if they were honoring the dead and faced the judge, the foreman of the jury kept their eyes on me, then she read it.

In the charge of first degree murder, we the jury, find Mr. Lamar Wright, not guilty.

My heart fell in my stomach; relief had filled my body. I felt like I could put this behind me and get back to my life my prayers had been answered.

In the second charge of possession of marijuana over the exceeded bolt, we the jury, find Mr. Lamar Wright, guilty.

Damn! I celebrated to soon.

Now is the time the jury speak on the reason of sentencing, please start when you are ready please, the judge said.

On count one, first degree murder, we acquit the defendant due to self-defense, we feel that they didn't come looking for trouble, but trouble came to find them!

And on count two! The judge said.

On count two, possession of marijuana over the exceeded bolt, we found the defendant guilty, because what he possessed were found in the home and could not been brought into the home, in the misted of a crime a lot of people lost their lives, because of what the defendant possessed.

Ok! What do the jury recommend on sentencing? we the jury ask that the defendant get the max on the punishment.

What the fuck just happen? And what the fuck do she mean that lives were lost because of me. What about the lives I saved? What about my mafuckin life being lost? She didn't give a fuck that I could have died! And now I know I'm going to prison for sure. To tell you the truth, I didn't speak another word or hear what the judge said after that until he said the time I would be receiving.

Mr. Lamar Wright, I sentence you to the Ohio Department of Corrections, for count 2 of the indictment for a term of 5 years.

Well damn now it's done, this is another chapter in my life I'm going to have to get through, when I looked back over my shoulder I could see May-so through the angry crowd that was mad at me for the lives that was lost and for the time I was receiving obviously they wanted more. My momma was crying out of control, while grandma Vickie rubbed her on her back to comfort her in this tough time. Those three people was all the family I had. When I looked at my grandma Vickie I could see the strength in her eyes, then I read her lips.

Keep your head up baby, I love you, you strong you can do this, believe me, everything is going to be alright, you're in the hands of God now.

Just for me to hear those words, my whole world stopped, I love you too!

The bailiff snatched me back into reality, Mr. Wright lets go right now! He forced me fast back behind the double doors and out of sight from everyone, a part of me went deep into a depression, I'm getting strip searched by the officers, and while I'm naked they are asking me all these stupid ass questions, in this moment I feel less than a man, you would too if another man is asking you to open your ass up so they could look inside. After that, I went through every emotion there is, each and every day and the feeling I couldn't shake the most was trapped, one of thC worst feelings in the world to have to stand up too. I laid in that lit up cell for the next two weeks and then they rode me to this place called C.R.C I'm glad I didn't have to stay in that place for long the C. O's would beat your ass for any and everything, the next place I was sent too was L.E.C.I also known as Lebanon Correctional Institution, as soon as I stepped in I could smell the death in the air. The process was long but after everything was done, they took me to my cell, and the cell was very small, you have to take turns on who's coming in stuck in a 12ft space, all cement so when it's summer time it gets so hot the walls sweat and there are no washer or dryers just clothes lines from wall to wall, all your clothes get washed by hand in a small trash can that they will sale you at the store, even the struggle ain't free! The roaches are bigger then the mice and they both are everywhere, this place is the jungle, you either stand for something or fall for anything, believe me in a place like this you will be tested, it's only a matter of time, that's why you don't get ready, you stay ready, and believe me I'm more than ready, when I slipped into my cell I noticed I had a celly, I didn't take to him at first, I had to fill him out but once I did he ended up being an alright guy. He called himself Chris-Chris, he ran with the Crips, over time I learned he was a real hot head, if he hears the wrong shit fly out your mouth and he would fly off the handle. As the time would fly by we became really close. Prison I found out is much like the streets besides there is no bitches unless they were CO's and another thing I found out was it was a whole lot of money that could be made, as soon as I got there I started making moves, getting my hand in the door where ever I could, I got cool with a couple kitchen workers and they would bring dope in for me from time to time. I moved into the big time when I met Mrs. Kathy Linn, her and her husband was both correctional officers and both have been for a while, her husbands was a real racist dick head, a real hard to approach type of guy but Mrs.

Kathy Linn was a real sweetheart, sexy as hell, looking for the attention her husband wasn't giving her and I had all the attention she needed. I couldn't keep my eyes off of her, she has a real natural sex appeal, the type you would eat up if it would fit in a bowl, it took me a while but I worked up the nerve to have a conversation with her and we ended up being friends, she has the look of a young Kim k or a Becky G, God she would always take my imagination to another place. When she would come to work, a lot of dudes would fight over the shower so they could watch her walk the range and pleasure themselves at the same time, they didn't care if they did it out in the open, they wanted her to watch, hoping she would see them and pick them as a choice. I did the opposite when it came to me I paid her no attention, shit why would I, she had enough people to give her that, so why waste my time, I never been the type to chase. What was crazy is, the more I didn't pay her any attention, the more she wanted me, the more she came around, I guess that's how her husband held on to her for this long. We talked on the cellphone that she brought me every night, that's when we had our little phone sex so I was able to learn her really well, all her desires and wants. I love when she would play with her pussy and deep throat her dildo on face time, then she would come to work and find time and ways to fuck me any and every place we could find. After a while people started watching our movements, these suckers' started running they mouth like bitches so her husband ended up catching word, we were messing around so he been all over me lately, shaken me down every chance he can get, just to get him off my tail I been having to make Mrs. Kathy Linn send me to the hole, which she hated because she couldn't see me as much but it was fair game for me because nobody would expect me to caught the pack back there in the hole but I did. See in prison everyone got their eyes on you, so in everything you do, you have to be slick because if anybody get word on how you moving, you are going to have to either battle with the gangs or deal with these dudes telling and the CO's kicking down the door in the middle of the night, when it came down to me Mrs. Kathy Linn, she kept me up on game, so I would know if they were on to me or not, in the mist of it all, the time was flying by 3 years had passed and I got a couple more years left to go, when me and Mrs. Kathy Linn wasn't doing our thing, I kept my ears to the streets, Mike D and Lil Will was doing they thang still in the streets, the whole joint kept they names in their mouth. I pretended I didn't *know* them every time someone would speak on them, because if it was any beef they had with them, they were going to have to face me. Lil Will would keep me laced with the pictures and he kept money on my books, but lately he has not been answering the phone, it took a couple of weeks for him to answer but when he did, our conversation was off, he told me he got into some shit, that he can't talk about on the recorded line, so we talked about a Lil bullshit here and there but as soon as the phone hung up I called him on the burner phone. He told me he had got into some beef on the other side of town and he had to shoot a mafucka and now he paralyzed from the waist down, pointing fingers and saying names, they locked up J Rob and Reese Butta so shit is already going crazy. Lil Will talked about how Reese Butta was ready to take the case so the heat don't fall on the team so he was standing tall but I Rob was breaking under pleasure, J Rob even told Lil Will that if he don't come get him out ofjail, he was going to tell the police everything, I was so surprised I just stared at the phone lost for words, J Rob and his brother Marky grew up in our little circle when we was kids, J Rob ran with us in the streets a little bit but most of the time he was under a tight watch, there mom would not allow to do nothing, they barely left there porch. Marky was the church going/ working type so it blew my mind when Lil Will said he been calling leaving threats, saying if Lil Will don't bond his brother out ofjail, he was going to kill him! When I heard that, I laughed and Lil Will got mad, I just tried my best to calm him down, because I knew deep down in my heart he was all talk, but Lil Will wasn't trying to hear that at all, so me and Lil Will hung up on bad terms, he told me prison made me sweet on beef, I didn't give a fuck what he was talking about, I just felt like maybe I just got to give him some space to clear his head, we all grew up together I know it will all work itself out eventually!

Rich Story:

After he got off the phone with Lamar, he had a fire burning in his stomach, he got back on the phone and called one of his top hit men T-Cottie, now T-Cottie was the type that will knock your head off in broad day light, without a thought, whatever Lil Will told him to do, he would do, he is a real quiet dude, one of them dudes that you had to watch, once you turn on the switch with him ain't no turning it off.

Hello,

What's up Lil Will what's good.

I need to take care of some business and I need you with me.

T-Cottie backed off the phone and smiled at the thought of the business, that needs his assistance.

You sure you need me and my assistance, T-Cottie asked as he smiled inside. Bro quit fuckin playing and pull up!

You sure now! This grown folk's business now!

Bro pull up! Lil Will said with a Lil anger in his voice.

Once Lil Will and T-Cottie got together they put the plan in place and then Lil Will made the call.

Hello,

Yo Marky this me Lil Will.

Man what the fuck do you want!

Bro chill, I'm calling to let you know we trying to bond your brother out but we need somebody with a job, we don't have no check stub and I know that you got a job can you go with us so we can go get him out.

Marky put in a long pause before the answer, why can't you find somebody else!

Listen I got the money, I'm doing my part, now it's time to do yours, damn it's yo brother! If you don't want to go get him, it's cool with me, I'll just keep my money or get him a lawyer or something.

Marky didn't want to be the reason his brother didn't get out so he agreed to go and help, but before he left the house he made it his business to tell his mom that he was going with Lil Will to bond his brother out, not only to tell her the good news, but because he also didn't trust Lil Will. After about an hour Lil Will finally called Marky back.

Marky meet me at the store around the corner from your house. Why you can't pick me up at the house you know the address!

Marky damn, what's up with all these questions, I'm getting my car detailed, just walk around the comer so we can go get this shit token care of.

Alright here I come, Marky said but something in his body didn't want him to move, he had a bad feeling about this all together, but another part of him felt like maybe he was tripping him and Lil Will grew up together and they got into many of fights and made up, so what he was feeling could be nothing, he brushed it off, kissed his mom and went out the door.

After they all met up, they shook hands and jumped in the car, while they were riding, joint after joint got rolled, then the bottle got passed around after they hit the liqueur store, shit went from a business move and now turned party. Marky started to feel like he had to start asking questions now.

Lil Will what's up? I thought we was going to bond my brother out?

Marky chill bro, we going to get him out we just wasting a Lil time T-Cottie said answering the question out of line.

Yeah we about to go meet up with these hoes for a minute, then we gone go meet up with the bail bondsman right after, I called him and he took my number and told me he will call me when he gets back in the office Lil Will said as he stared at Marky though the rearview mirror.

Marky sat back in his seat and stared out the window, as the wind hit his face, he could feel the weed and the drink taking over his body, he hasn't felt this good in a long time, him and Lil Will use to do this all the time back in the days when he would sneak out mom's house in the middle of the night, he just smiled because it felt good, it felt like old times.

Meanwhile T-Cottie was watching him through the rearview mirror, pretending to put the bottle to his lips, watching the focus drain from Marky body sip after sip, Lil Will bent the corner down a dead end street.

Man where the fuck is we going, this a dead end fool! Marky said looking for answers.

4"his is the street that the Lil hoes live down, chill and don't be acting crazy when you go in these hoes house either! Lil Will said trying to calm Marky down.

Out of nowhere a guy jumped out and started flagging down the car. Lil Will Lil Will a bro stop! I need a ride! Stop bro!

Lil Will pulled over.

What the fuck is you doing? Why you picking him up! Said T-Cottie.

Lil Will was starting to lose his footing and let the guy Ron-Ron into the car, it was clear at this point to T-Cottie that Lil Will was ready to back out of the plan and he wasn't going for that. T- Cottie game mode came with no off button, once he gets started it wasn't no turning around, so he decided to take control of the situation all together.

Yeah this the street the Lil hoe Candy stay down and I'm sure she got some friends so he could come too!

Bro I thought you was going to take me downtown, I got a couple moves to bust that can't wait, fuck some bitches' bro!

Man you jumped in the car with us, so you going where we going, ain't no getting out so enjoy the ride mafucka!

Ron-Ron watched his every word through his eyes in the rearview mirror, not wanting to argue, he sat back and shut his mouth, he heard about T-Cottie, about how he got down in the streets, just being around this dude made him uncomfortable. Him and Lil Will had always been cool, but if he would of knew T-Cottie was in the car he wouldn't have even stopped them, damn he even wondered what was Lil Will even doing with this dude, he was starting to get a crazy feeling something wasn't right about them being together.

Man! Come on! Are we there yet? I have to piss bad as hell! Marky said as he rocked back and forth in the back seat.

Chill! We almost there damn, you keep acting like a big ass kid Marky! You ain't the only one who got to piss! Marky said.

The street was long and dark, and there were houses on the street but most of them were abandon.

Have you ever been over here before? This shit seems like a set up if I ain't seen one Ron-Ron said as he stared out the window.

Man shut up! You just acting like a pussy we straight, I been over here plenty of times. She just stays in the cut that's all, Lil Will pull in this drive way she stays all the way in the back.

As Ron-Ron looked around every part of him, just wanted to get out and run, but the emotion of everything going on had him froze.

Fuck this shit let me out right here I got to piss, Marky opened the door, got out and ran to the nearest bushes to relieve himself. T-Cottie followed behind as if he had to use the bathroom as well.

Lil Will didn't move, the whole time he kept his head in his phone not saying a word, which was not like him.

Lil Will what's up man, is something on your mind?

Before he could look up or even answer me, all I heard was Pop! Pop! Pop! When I looked out the window to see where the shots was coming from, Marky had took off running with his pants halfway down, trying to get away from T-Cottie, I reached for the door to makC a move to escape only to see that the child lock was put on my side of the door so I would have to climb out the window if I wanted to get out, when I looked back out the window T-Cottie was standing over Marky dropping shot after shot into his face until the clip emptied then he reached in his back pocket for another clip and started heading towards the car leaving Marky lifeless body in a pool of blood, I was trapped and the only thing left I could do is make a plea for my life.

Lil Will I didn't see nothing, just let me go I promise I won't tell a soul about this, come on man! I don't have nothing to do with this!

Lil Will lifted his head from the phone and into the rearview mirror into the back seat at Ron-

Ron.

Bro you cool, just chill out, roll up this joint!

Lil Will went into the glove box to get the weed, as T-Cottie was jumping back into the car.

Ron-Ron tried to hurry up and speak his peace to T-Cottie to assure him a word of this will never get out to anyone, he just needed him to trust him.

Lil Will what the fuck you doing? Why you ain't got rid of him yet!

Before Lil Will could answer, T-Cottie let off a shot in the back seat striking Ron-Ron in the face.

Noooo! What is you doing? He ain't got shit to do with this, Lil Will screamed at T-Cottie. You stupid mafucka, you think we gone let him live after what he just saw!

What the fuck you mean we, you did this!

O no brother it's we! We bonded by blood, either you shoot him or I'm gone be the only one going home tonight! T-Cottie while keeping his eye on Lil Will every movement.

Will please help me! Ron-Ron pleaded as the blood filled up in his eyes.

Lil turned to Ron-Ron, I'm sorry bro, you just picked the wrong night for a ride! Shoot'em screamed T-Cottie.

Lil Will let off a shot into his chest, throwing him back into his seat, then he jumped out and dragged Ron-Ron from the back seat as he fought like hell to breath, he stood over him putting two more shots into him, watching for signs of movement and once it was none, he jumped back into the car and drove off. After he dropped T-Cottie off at his spot, all types of thoughts had started to overpower his brain, some were fear, but mostly guilt and regret, but what was done was done. Now it was all about covering his tracks from this point on, so he pulled out his phone and made a call to Marky's mom, it rung two times and then she answered.

Hello! Hello! Who is this!

How you doing Ms. Johnson, this is Will, I was calling to tell you, that if Marky don't bond J Rob out tomorrow, that I can help, if you need me, so just let me know, this is my number if you want to get in touch with me.

Ok baby, thank you, I'll do that!

Ok talk to you later, Lil Will said just as he was about to hang up, Ms. Johnson called out to him. Will! Will!

Yes, ma'am.

Have you seen or talked to Marky today? I been trying to reach him for a while now! He paused before he answered, no ma'am I haven't talked to him all day.

Ok, if you talk to him, tell him to call me ok!

For Lil Will the morning had come fast, even dough he got no sleep, all he could do is stare at the wall all night. Once he got up and rolled up his joint, he checked his missed calls, he had over a hundred on his phone, at least 90 came from T-Cottie, even dough he didn't want to, he hit him back anyway.

Yea what's up bro?

Man why the fuck you ain't answering the phone? You need to turn on the news, that mafucka Ron-Ron ain't dead! It's on every channel!

As soon as I turned on the TV the news anchor was telling the story:

Two people was shot last night in the Walnut Hills area, in the 3200 block, between Kemper and Lane Street. Mark Johnson 23 years old was found dead on the scene, the other man's name is Ronald Smith 20 years old, is in the hospital under critical condition with very serious injuries, authorities ask for everyone to come together and say a prayer in hopes that Mr. Smith will through, not only for his life but also so they could get some answers for the family of Mr.

Johnson in this tragic situation. When I talked to the doctors, they said with his condition, there is just no way of knowing just yet if he will pull through, we will make sure we keep you updated on the story, I'm Tricia Mackie and this is channel 9 WLWT News.

Every word spoken, fell on my soul, if he lives, I know for a fact, he would make it his business to become a state's witness, all types of thoughts put in work on my mind, damn this the type of dude who don't live by the street code, shit most of these dudes don't even know what that is! At this point finishing what I started, was more important than the air I breathe! But until then I have to keep shit normal and keep shit normal is exactly what I did, I helped Marky mom raise the funeral money, she didn't have enough money to bury him, we did all types of shit to get that money from cookouts to t-shirt sales! Damn near on every comer and because the respect they had for me and my team, there were a lot of people who came out to support the cause. After I collected everything I gave his mom about a quarter of the money. Which she was glad to get, but it was the look in her eyes, that kind of put my heart in a panic. It was like she could see through me. A strong unspoken word stood between us. After I gave her the money she stepped in for a hug and after we was locked tight in our embrace she whispered in my ear.

The people who did this to my son! I spoke, yea!

They are going to pay for what they did! Not because he was my son, no! no! no! but because he was an innocent soul and God wages war for all his children, why they killed him is something that I may never know or understand. Even if I knew who did this, her grip got tighter as she continued to speak.

I would forgive them and stand back and let God take over, God said vengeance is mine. Then she kissed me on the cheek, told me to take care and walked away. I talked to a couple more people then I got in the car and drove away watching my surroundings as we leave the curve.

Marky Mom:

Right after she let Lil Will go, she could feel the sickness building up in her stomach. Her mind was all over the place. A lot of people been telling her that Lil Will and T-Cottie was the ones who had something to do with her son getting killed. What had her so threw off, was the fact that Lil Will had helped her with burying her son and calling her day and night pushing for justice for him, and not even once did he seem like he could of did this! When she pushed her thoughts around the one that always seem to hit the surface the most, is what Marky said before he left her house for the last time, besides him telling her he loved her, he also said that Lil Will was coming to pick him up so they could go bond out his brother and she knew he would not lie to her and then she remembered something else that seem weird about that night, and that was when Will called her and said if Marky don't bond Rob out I'll get him out. She started putting all the pieces together, then she called the detectives and told them all the information she had about her son case. After she got off the phone with the detectives, she felt like now she could take a step back and let God do the rest, there were nothing else left for her to do.

The Detectives:

After Detective Rainwater got off the phone with Mark Johnson's mother he was over showered with joy, there was finally a strong break in the case and now we have a clue on who might have something to do with this, as he looked at the screen with burned out eyes from getting no sleep for the last week in a half, he had been tied to the case, everything about the case broke his heart. He figured the best thing he could do is get some answers for Mr. Johnson mother, he looked up the two names that was given to him, William Blake and Todd Campbell. Todd Campbell had a record but William Blake didn't, after checking Mark Johnson's phone records it showed that William Blake had been in communication with Mark all day, calls and text messages furthering the evidence that Mark's mother gave me, so he wrote up a report to further investigate the suspects of the case. A Detective accompanied him to the hospital to check out the condition of the witness. As soon as he got there he was approached by a nurse with a look of worry on her face.

Detective Rainwater and Detective Cooper I'm glad that you are here, it's not looking too good for Mr. Smith, our nurse has had to sit with him all night, his condition is seeming to become worse.

Is he going to make it? Said Detective Cooper.

Right now it's hard to tell, he keeps slipping in and out of consciousness and when he is with us, it's like he is in a bad dream.

What do you mean?

It's like he is fighting somebody off, and he keeps saying over and over Lil Will don't do this! I think that's something you need to look into, whoever Lil Will is.

As soon as she said the name Lil Will, he thought about William Blake, it was like a light bulb had went off in his head. Even dough he didn't have a complete witness statement he had enough for an arrest warrant as long as he could get Mr. Smith on record, right as they were in the middle of talking a medical emergency came over the loud speaker for Mr. Smith's Room.

I have to go Detectives, Mr. Smith is crashing, I have to get to him but I'll keep you up to date and just like that she was gone.

The detectives rushed out the building to put the arrest warrant in place, it was time for him to pay William Blake aka Lil Will a visit.

Lil Will:

As Lil Will stepped into the church all eyes were on him, their eyes filled with disgust, in his heart he knew he shouldn't be here but that would be out of place of normal. So he went up front as close as he could to the casket, to pay a sick respect for the dead. He closed his eyes and asked God for forgiveness. The words of Marky's mom kept playing in his head over and over again, making him feel bad about everything, because deep down he knew that Marky didn't deserve what happen to him but it was a part of the game that comes with being in the streets, as he sat there with his eyes closed he could feel somebody walk up next to him. When he opened his eyes it was T-Cottie staring at him.

What's up bro!

What's up! What are you doing here?

Shit! What you thought I was going to miss this, (laughing out loud). Be quite! have some respect!

Have some respect, for who! This Sucka, who got his ass killed for making bad choices, the choice of fuckin with me! I'll be back, I'm about to go view the body and get a pic for my collection, every since my first, I like to keep record, this ain't my first funeral and believe me Lil Will this won't be my last.

When he left me a chill flowed through my body, not from fear, let's just say when he is in the room you can feel his cold presence, death laid on his soul. It became clear to me, it was his life's mission to destroy you in any way he could and I could tell it has got bad to the point, he can't tell his friends from his foes, any and everybody is becoming fair game, and in those type of situations, it's only a matter of time before he turns on you. So ı knew I had to keep my guard up, after the viewing of the body, the service started, T-Cottie tried to get me to leave but I dismissed him, I needed to be here and I didn't feel like dealing with him at all, it wasn't no telling what he had up his sleeve. After I put my focus back on grabbing a peace of mind, the service started and the preacher started preaching and I swear it felt like he was talking to me the whole time.

The preacher:

Today I want to speak out of the bible Micah chapter 7 verse 5, put no trust in a neighbor, have no confidence in a friend; guard the doors of your mouth from her who lies in your embrace, I want to talk about trust! Because the lord touched me today to speak about just that, trust! Trust is what costed this young man to lose his life. Now I don't know any details about the case, but I knew him personally, so I knew his heart, good guy, God fearing guy, would give you the shirt off his back if you need it, real respectful, he was a member of this church, not just some thug that died in the streets to some drug deal gone bad! No! he was a real hard worker with a future in front of him, but trust ended his life shorter then it needed to, who did this could have been a friend, family member, an ally, etc. and we don't know who or which one, but what we do know is he trusted them.

Every word the preacher spoke, set a fire to my bones, it was as if everyone knew, even the preacher and he was talking directly to me, eye to eye, his stare never moving from its place. The more I stayed the more I began to get filled with guilt, I had to leave I couldn't take it no more, so I lower my head to avoid all eye contact as I made my way out of the church, when I headed out the door, I notice two men sitting in a black unmarked car and when they saw me, they jumped out the car and started heading my way. I never seen them before so they couldn't know me, but they are moving like they do, as they got closer, I stopped in place to watch their movement and one stopped in front of me and the other slightly behind, it became clear they were trying to corner me in.

Mr. William Blake I'm Detective Rainwater with the Cincinnati homicide unit and I have a warrant for your arrest for the connection in the murder of Mark Johnson and the assault on Ronald Smith!

My heart dropped, damn they got me, I don't know how and at this point I'm not sure if it even matter, what matters now is making it out of this situation, as the Detectives was walking me to the car, the church was letting out, everyone watching and yelling in a rage, screaming things five minutes ago they didn't have the nuts to say and then I saw Marky's mom walk out the church and up to me and the Detectives.

May I speak with him, she said to the Detectives, they rolled down my window. Yes, ma'am go right ahead.

Will baby I don't know what happen, and I'm asking you for me and my peace of mind, to just let me know why, what did he do to deserve this? As she spoke to me, the tears flowed from her eyes, I wanted to tell her my place, but she wouldn't understand, that even dough I had love for her son, it wasn't enough to choose his life over mines, I closed my eyes and never spoke a word, she stood up and the look in her eyes was far from anger, the look in her eyes, stood for something different, as if she was sorry for me and then she said, I told you the lord said vengeance is mine! What was in the dark, has shown his face in the light today, and still I forgive you and right after the last word rolled off her tongue, she was gone, the car rolled off on its way to take me to the county jail.

Lamar:

After calling around for a while getting no answer from Lil Will, I decided to call Mike D. he told me everything that happen with the murder and it really hurt my heart! Not just for Lil Will but for Marky as well, we all grew up together, no way Marky should have died with his pants down to his ankles and especially by the hands of us, a friend, it really made me wonder if he could of did this type of shit to me, I ain't gone lie, the news put me in a really bad mood, so I went back to my cell and rowed up a couple ofjoints, turned on my music and zoned out, I didn't want to be bothered, but that didn't last long, even that got interrupted.

Lil Wright! Lil Wright! Lil Wright! Man what the fuck do you want?

Man bro I need to holla at you!

I sat up on my bed and gave him the attention he was looking for, his face was covered in worry, like cheap make-up on a dirty bitch, it was written all over his face.

What's going on? Holla at me!

Man bro this dude rode in from another camp claiming he know you and been asking where he could find you! Shit he even passing out money to the first person who could bring him your location.

And who the fuck is this?

I don't know him, I think he said his name was Skep Dollar, he didn't act like he had beef with you or anything, he said y'all was real tight, do you know him?

As soon as I heard Dollai name, my mind began to race, I knew the only reason he could be looking for me was to get his revenge, and I don't blame him, shit I would be mad to if I got set up to take the fall on 5 bodies, so I decided to throw the messager off to buy me some time.

O yea I know who that is, that's a good friend of mine!

Ok! So you want me to tell him where you at then, he said as he searched my eyes for the answer.

Naw, don't do that! I want to surprise him, tell him I got caught up on some bullshit and you think they about to ride me to another prison.

His face was full of confusion, but he agreed to do what I wanted and walked away. Immediately I put a plan in place, for the next couple of weeks I laid low. I didn't even go eat at the chow hall, I didn't want to show my face at all, I got all my information through the messager, my celly at the time Chris-Chris I learned was a hot head, all he wanted to do was either fight, get high, or be in the middle of somebody else drama. He was a real crash out and when I thought about it, that is something I could use to my advantage, something I could use against Skep Dollar, so when me and Chris-Chris was alone, daily I would plant my seeds in his head.

Yo Chris-Chris when I went to rec I heard this dude keep talking about you, he, Who! Who! Who the fuck was talking about me?

Listen damn! You won't even let me get the words out!

With just the little words I said, Chris-Chris began to pace the floor, building in anger with every word, searching my face for the answers.

Bro you need to calm down and let me tell you what happen!

Chris-Chris slowed down his pace and went in the direction of the chair across the room, once he sat down and gave me his full attention, I continued in what I had to say.

Ok like I said when I was in rec I heard this dude speaking on your name. What's his name? he said.

I heard one of the guys call him Skep Dollar, any way y'all supposed to have some beef from the pass and he wanted get at you on it!

O yeah, is that right, shit I ain't hiding, why the fuck he ain't pulled up on me yet?

I don't know, but I don't think he gone confront you, he looks like the type of guy who just sends hits.

The look in his face went from anger to worry.

I got to get ahead of this, I can't let nobody sneak up on me, you got to show me who he is!

Listen! Don't worry I got your back, I'm gone do more than show you who he is bro, I got a plan that's going to end him for good!

We sat down and put the plan together, the only other thing next to do was execute. Lil Will:

As Lil Will sat in the courtroom, he had a lot of thoughts cross through his mind, he couldn't believe how he got caught up in all this bullshit, T-Cottie was now his co-defendant not because he told but because the stupid motherfucker actually told on himself, he caught a gun case riding around in a dope fiend rental with no license, they sent him to prison for that, and then when he hit the yard and he started telling everybody about the murder, he called home and spoke about it on a recorded line, they played it for everybody to hear in court, lie even had the nerve to say I was the one who put him up to it, day after day, people I knew would get up on the stand, talking about what they think happened, my lawyer would tell me I'm in good shape, I just didn't know how, through my eyes, shit was looking like it was only getting worse but all he kept saying was, William we can beat this, they still haven't shown no real solid evidence! I didn't know anything about that, all I could do is trust him, I had no other choice or money, I gave him all I had, he had my life in his hands. The prosecutor walked over to my lawyer and whispered something in his ear, and my lawyer got up and dismissed himself from the table to talk to the prosecutor in private. I had a bad feeling something was wrong, plus when my lawyer did shit in private with the opposition, it always made me feel like I was in this room alone and that they both, were working together against me. I never felt so damn trapped in my life, as I was pulling my head from my hands, my lawyer was sitting down next to me, then he leaned in as close as he could, like he didn't want to share his words with another soul, those words were only for me.

William we got a problem!

Damn I didn't want to hear this shit, before I could process this shit the prosecutor started walked to the door so he can call in his next witness for the state.

Ronald Smith, come to the front, the prosecutor shouted out the door.

Fuck! Ron-Ron had pulled through after all, the last I heard about him, he wasn't even conscious, eating through a straw, not doing to good and his family was making plans to pull the plug, because it was killing them financially, but it all was a lie, and I now know that for sure, the prosecutor helped his mom, roll him to the stand in his wheelchair, every juror placed there attention on him, at that moment, I knew my life was over, from the first word spoken to the last, the emotion over powered the whole court room, he painted a vivid picture of that night, the night I so desperately wanted to put behind me, was now the master of my fate, I was the bad guy, covered in blood, blood that another man caused and nobody would listen to my side, even if I told it, I had a chance to stop all of this, but I couldn't, it was him or should I say them or me, if I would of said no or that I wanted out, they would have been burying me right along with them, after he was finish speaking, everybody who looked at me, looked at me like a monster laying under their babies bed. I knew this situation was far from good. The jury went in the back for deliberations, to decide how my life will turn out, they stayed in the back, all for about 30 minutes before they came back out to deliver the verdict.

All rise,

The judge began to speak:

I'm sure the jury has had enough time to look over all the evidence to make a strong and fair decision in this case.

Yes, your honor!

Ok, what did the jury decide?

Me and the jury decide that we find William Blake guilty of all charges!

The whole courtroom jumped to their feet and began to cheer, like I just ran in for a touchdown, excited to share the moment to the end of my life, right after the jury, the judge was ready to pass down the sentence.

Mr. William Blake the State of Ohio has found you guilty of all charges, please stand as I pass down the sentence.

I could feel me losing the strength in my legs, my heart was beating at an uncontrollable rate, the whole time the judge spoke he never looked me in the eyes until he spoke his last words.

Mr. William Blake,

His eyes looked as if he was looking through me, a chill covered my whole body.

On the charge of First Degree Murder, I sentence you to life in prison without the possibility of parole.

After those words, my heart had stopped in its place, the next thing I remember is I was waking up on the floor of the courtroom, the judge was still delivering the sentence like the fall never happen, the judge passed down another life sentence for Ron-Ron because he said his life would never be the same, after that, nothing else mattered my whole soul had become vacate, fuck that rat bitch Ron-Ron, and they say his life would never be the same, what about my life? After they locked me in the holding cell I felt the walls closing in. overpowered by my thoughts, I felt a deep remorse for what I did come over me, so I began to put it all on paper, I wrote a letter to my brother and mom, then I wrote a letter to Marky's mom, giving her the answers she was looking for and hoping she could forgive me, it was only right she knew the truth about that night. Even after the pen stopped, the weight of my soul, held me down, I loosen my shoe strings and began to take off my clothes, I could feel the heat rising, feeling like a blaze just hit the room, I stepped onto a chair to escape the heat flowing through the cell, the higher I got, the more relief I was starting to feel, I don't want to hurt any more, before I knew it, I was tied in place and taking a step in a new direction. I could feel the pain drain from my body, I just closed my eyes until all the pain was gone.

Lamar:

Things was finally starting to fall in place for me, Chris-Chris had put the Crips on alert about Skep Dollar, now even dough he had a hit out on me, I wasn't bothered, May-so always told me that a mafucka can't hit what they can't see, just keep moving and keep moving is just what I did, along with changing my appearance to not be easily spotted in a crowd. I kept feeding the birdy's miss information to keep dude spent, I have to make a move soon, every since this beef with Skep Dollar been in front of me, I stopped everything even the way I caught sleep, it's hard to sleep when someone want you dead, it's been a lot going on so I had not reached out to home in a minute. I got a letter from Mike D telling me to call him, and that it was important! I got that letter about a month ago, I ain't been having nothing going on, so I didn't feel the need to hit him up, I heard through the grape vine that Lil Will and T-Cottie both got double life, I figured that might be what Mike D want to tell me. I wonder what prison they sent Lil Will too, so I could pull a couple of strings together to make sure he comfortable if nothing else. Then I bumped into T-Cottie myself, he was reckless and all over the place, he couldn't keep eye contact for more than 5 seconds, the mafucka didn't waste no time, in dipping his dick in them punks, as soon as he hit the yard, with no shame in his game, he put it out in the open,

I had to pull down on him, to see what the fuck his problem is!

A T-Cottie what's up bro? Lil Wright is that you fool?

Man cut the shit! What the fuck you got going on? Running around here holding hands with another man?

He laughed at me like he just heard the funniest joke told in the world. T-Cottie! Does it look like I'm fucking joking man?

Lil Wright you must ain't heard, huh?

Heard what! That you got double life or that you been a fag? Seems like you free of an excuse to pull it out to the world now!

Yo! You can say what you want but I'm gone die in here screaming fuck the world, knocking these fags down one at a time, and at least I didn't kill myself like a coward like Lil Will did!

In that minute, the world had stopped, I waited for the laugh he had when I questioned his man hood, but he gave me nothing as I searched his eyes.

O you didn't know huh? They found him butt naked hung up on the wall, dick out, eyes open, with shit running down his leg, they examined his ass because they thought somebody fucked him and put him there, but I guess he fucked himself all alone.

On his last word I rushed him before the smile could even form on his face, I lifted him off his feet with all I had in me, cutting off his air supply, the tighter I made my grip, I looked for the fear in his eyes, I wanted him to plead for his life, I had no intention of letting him go until there were no more life left in his worthless body, for a moment my vision had changed and I felt like I floated to a different place. The only thing that snapped me back in place was the CO's shamming me to the floor, as I tried to stand, they fought to keep me down.

Stay down motherfucker! Stay the fuck down!

They beat me with their Billy clubs to bring order to the situation, but to tell you the truth, at that moment, everything in me was numb, I could not feel a thing, it took me a while but about time I came to and begin to feel like myself again, I was in the hole, trying to keep warm from the broken windows, one eye closed shut, four broken ribs and a broken heart from the news, I didn't want to eat I just watched either the birds eat it or the rats that ran free through the walls, I was in hell! I laid still because the pain had become unbearable, the dim light shines in the hallway just enough where I could see a figure approaching me at a slow pace, I couldn't move if I wanted to.

Well! Well! Well! Look what the fuck we have here! All this time I thought mafucka's was lying when they said your ass was in the hole, I just had to come see for myself!

Just from the voice, I knew exactly who it was, Skep Dollar, we had finally crossed paths and the only thing between us was the bars I sat on the other side of.

Lil Wright it's been a long time since we last seen each other you rat motherfucker!

Rat! Lol check that shit at the door! I ain't get on no stand and tell on nobody, so you can miss me with that shit!

True! True! But I did here the 911 caller, when I was at trial and it did sound just like you! Fuck you Skep!

Naw Fuck you, and you might as well have got on the stand, you abandon me and set me up with Money Mo mom and daughter bodies, yeah I ain't stupid I knew it was you! It took me a minute to put it together but I did, I bet you fuckin thought I was stupid huh?

Obviously you fuckin are! Lol if I think!

Think what! That you couldn't had put this together, had me go for the dummy bag while you go get the real one! All these years and you didn't send me shit and it don't matter, fuck the money boy, I want to drain the fuckin life from your body then we will be even!

And how the fuck you gone do that? You think I'm just gone lay here and let you kill me?

You can't stay in here forever, just know when they let you out in a couple days I'll be here waiting for you!

And just like that, he turned his back on me and walked away. Sure of himself and his plan to end my life. I ain't gone lie, those next couple of days was rough, I didn't eat or sleep, scared he might either poison me or find favor with the guards. Most of the guards could be paid off to turn their heads, so I had to stay on point, once I was released they sent me back to my old block, everyone seemed to be happy I was back T-Cottie gay ass got shook and moved to F-block, where he could swing and dip his dick freely. I quickly gave up on chasing T-Cottie, I had bigger fish to fry and it was time to finish Skep Dollar once and for all. As soon as I seen Chris-Chris, he was all ears on what needed to happen next.

Lil Wright bro, what's the word, bro is you ok? It looks like you been smoking crack back that bitch, you need me to hit you off with a soup or something?

Yeah shit! I do need that shit! Man that nigga Skep Dollar was laying on me while I was in the hole, threaten me, and he said he was going to kill me the first chance he gets!

What! How the fuck he knows you when I'm the one he wants? Unaware of our history, I stayed far from the truth.

Because he found out we was tight and now he wants to make me out to be an example. O yeah, and he told you that?

Hell yeah, you know these mafucka's like to run they mouth, man Chris-Chris, this mafucka is reckless, we got to get this dude out the way before he catches one of us slipping!

The look in Chris-Chris eyes looked as if I had set a fire, he walked off without saying another word, I laid back in the cut, watching him from a distance as he rounded up all the Crips, I knew what I needed done was now in motion, I got up and went to the phone to make a call to Mike D, just to check on him but he didn't answer, I called a couple other people who run in his circle and they told me he ain't been doing to good every since Lil Will took his life, damn! A part of me wish it wasn't true, I wish he would have at least come and talked to me, I would of gave him the best advice I had. More time passed, for the next couple of days, the pain from my broken ribs was still hard to bear, but even through the pain, I began to work out, I had to get ready for a war after my workout I got real tired, I felt like I ain't had no sleep in months, as soon as my head hit my pillow, it wasn't long on this night before reality came to a dream.

Wake the fuck up mafucka! I want to see your eyes before I kill your bitch ass!

I opened my eyes, to see Skep Dollar standing in the distance and one of his goons standing over me, with a knife to my throat, I was far from safe on the one night I needed to be.

What the fuck you waiting for kill that mafucka! Skep Dollar screamed to the top of his lungs.

As his goon, pulled the knife from my neck, he drew in a motion to stab me in the chest, I did the only thing I could do was fight, the commotion woke Chris-Chris up, evening out the fight, the goon was smooth with the knife, sticking me in places I didn't know he had landed, my heart was racing and all I could think about was not losing my life, with every punch I threw, I threw it as if it was my last, blow after blow I could see Skep Dollar goon losing his legs from my power, my punches crushing him and his ability to swing, I began to overpower him, throwing him around the room like a rag doll, I had to hurry, while Chris-Chris was putting up a good fight, Skep Dollar was still in control of the fight, I wrested the knife from the goons hand with all my might, then stabbed him over and over again in the face until I could see his life slowly slip away from him, as Skep Dollar goon fell to the side, his eyes glazed over with a stuck expression of shock in his eyes, as lie fell over, I stepped over him to join the fight between Chris-Chris and Skep Dollar. Chris-Chris had taken a blow causing him to drop to his knees, out of nowhere a blade was pulled out Skep Dollar back pocket, I rushed him, swinging in the same motion, we both landed at the same time, Skep Dollars blade landed in the temple of Chris-Chris ending his fight, mines landed into Skep Dollar neck, knocking off his feet sending him into the corner of the cell, I quickly ran and got on top of him, stabbing him so many times, I painted the door, the walls and the floor with his blood, one thing I knew for sure is that I wasn't letting him survive this fight, I had to end this today, I didn't stop, shit I couldn't stop, I was truly in another world, far from where I was standing, the guards stood amazed by the mess that were made. Once I realize all that happen was over and returned to my rightful place in life, I began to feel weak, I didn't notice all the blood I had lost from being stabbed by the goon multiple times, I fainted on the floor before the CO's could even approach with force I had nothing left, I died over and over again on the way to the hospital, in and out of a dream with everyone who fell victim to me surrounding my bed, waiting on me to cross over, the only one fighting them off for me was Lil Will, he was naked, mouth closed, eyes wide open, but I could hear his voice over the others.

Get up Lamar! You have to fight, get up Lamar, you have to fight!

And fight is what I did, with everything I had in me, I fought to breathe, through the electrical shock I came to life on the doctors table, pulling out IV's determine to stand up, but as soon as I stood I fell on my face, in pain but I'm alive! The war between me and Skep Dollar was finally over, he didn't survive and neither did Chris-Chris, he laid in the hospital fighting for months, nothing changed in his condition, due to their financial situation they had to pull the plug. Even dough I wasn't in a gang, the Crips embrace me for fighting with him to the end, there was no charges filed against me for murdering Skep Dollar and his goon because there should not have been a way for this to happen with me laying in a cell behind a locked door, a couple of CO's got fired and a strong investigation had got started, the word in the joint was they was supposed to come in and straight kill me in my sleep and frame Chris-Chris for it all. It didn't go down that way because of all that talking but I can't help to reflect on, the what ifs, the rest of my bit in the joint was smooth, I was well protected, I got the pack in and continued to run up my bag. Every since the incident with Dollar, I been thinking about starting a family and settling down, it took me to die on that table and get brought back to life, to truly want to change. I did the rest of my time and when it was time, they opened the door for me, and with that I truly felt blessed, because I left some real mafucka's behind. Who ain't never going home! I had to keep them on my mind and most of all in my heart. Everything felt different on the other side of the fence, the smell of the air, even the touch of the sun, Mike D was waiting for me when I came out.

Yo! Yo! Yo! Yoooo! What's up bro! Mike D said as he was barely able to stand.

I could tell that he was happy to see me, but I could tell in his body language, he was still overwhelmed with stress, from losing his brother, he was far from the old Mike D I know, he reeked of piss and liquor, and had lost a whole bunch of weight, though I tried to hide the way I was feeling, it blead right through my face.

Come on bro! why you looking at me like that? he said Like what?

Like you discussed with me or something!

I was lost for words; I really didn't know what to say. I never seen him in this type of state of mind, the whole ride home he kept talking about, how he need to get the streets back poppin and that he been waiting on me to lock all the blocks down, what he didn't know is that I'm done, the streets might as well have been a foreign land to me, that I have no desire to even visit.

Man we got to hit the club tonight bro! go see some bitches throw that ass around! He said with excitement in his eyes.

Yeah! It's been a while since I had some good pussy, I most definitely got to get this big mafucka emptied out.

We both laughed and just for a moment it was just like old times.

When I got home, I just wanted to relax before me and Mike D hit the club, so I took me a nap, got up hit the mall so my style could be up to date and then I hit Mike D on his line, and just like I thought he was drunk out of his mind, so I spent him for tonight, because I'm not in the mood to babysit a fuckin grown man, after I got off the phone with Mike D, I looked online to see what spot would be jumping tonight, and club 360 popped up, so I got the directions and made my way there, when I got there I could not believe my eyes, it was so many woman everywhere, all types of shapes and sizes, my heart and my dick was having a fight on who was gone jump out first, I hurried and parked the car, I couldn't wait to get inside the building, as soon as I got through the door, the music was so loud I could barely hear myself think, I went to the bar and grab me a drink, then I laid watch in the corner, to watch everything that was going on around me, it's crazy how much had changed since I been locked up in prison, the whole night I was feeling real out of place, until this sexy white chick crossed my path, it was something about her that really turned me on. Before prison, I wouldn't even have passed a thought about fucking with a white chick, I was racist at heart and I didn't even know it, but once I got caught up in them porno books, I got addicted to that pretty pink pussy, I could imagine all the things I would love to do once I got one, I just had to test that out and my guys use to always tell me they had the best head in the world, the whole time I was eyeing her, she was doing the same, she had a smile that could light up the room, a real nasty walk, sandy red hair, the cutest freckles, a nice fat wide ass, that looked like as soon as she bend it over, her whole pussy would jump out at you, I had to get at her, I waited for the right time, then I caught her at the bar.

Hey what's up snow bunny how you doing?

I'm good and you, she said while checking me out from head to toe.

Can I get you something to drink as well as get to know you in the process? Huh?

You heard me pink toe, can I get to know you, starting with your name!

What's up with all these pet names? Snow bunny and pink toe, my name is Sarah and what took you so long to come talk to me?

Lol what you mean baby?

You act like you ain't been watching me all night, stalking me, like you ready to take the pussy or something.

We both laughed but I moved in closer, so we can share the same space. Well you know I just got out the joint, this my first day out.

What is the joint?

She acted as if she didn't know, what I was talking about, but at the same time her eyes lit up like she was a kid in the candy shop, it was evident where her mind had landed.

Prison? I said checking for her reaction.

Ok so you a bad boy huh? You ain't gone hurt me or something is you? Naw I ain't gone hurt you!

We continued to talk all through the night, then we exchanged numbers, and as soon as we were leaving each other, she called me on the phone and we talked some more, she was really easy to talk too, I felt like I have known her all my life. From the way she talked I could tell she didn't want to get off the phone, so I cut out all the bullshit and asked her did she want to come stay with me, to my surprise and with no hesitation she said yes! It took her a while to arrive at my house but when she did, all I could say was ole my God, she had her sandy red hair down to her shoulders and when the light hit it I could see just a touch of blonde, she stood about 5'6" 135 pounds in a tan trench coat and red hills, the trench coat barely covered her ass, it wasn't hard to tell, she had nothing on underneath. The way she walked up demanded attention, when she didn't have to, demand anything, whatever she wanted, I would of gave to her, damn! She had me at hello.

Hi baby,

Good morning, I thought since I kept you up all night, from running my mouth, the least I could do is cook you some breakfast, she said as she leaned in a gave me a slow passionate kiss.

Baby I don't have much food; I still have to go to the grocery store.

Don't worry about that, I got some groceries for you in the car, they were too heavy, so you got to go get them.

She handed me the keys to her car and walked on into the house, I walked down to the car and looked inside for the groceries, but there were none in sight, just a small bag of fruit and a fresh bottle of whip cream, after I also searched the trunk of the car and there still was no site of the groceries, I grabbed the bag of fruit and proceeded to enter the house and ask questions, I looked all around the house and couldn't find Sarah anywhere, I know she had not left, I still had her keys to the car, the only place left to check was my bedroom, as soon as I entered, the site of her instantly made me lose my mind, she had laid plastic all over the bed, along with a couple of bath towels, like she knew shit was about to get real messy, her legs lay all the way to the back of her head, straps attached to her ankles, connected to the bed, keeping her in place, exposing her fat pretty pink pussy in the air, and to take the cake, she even put her ass on a plate, showing me just what she expected of me, I could feel my dick, overpowering its way through my draws, trying to find an escape route out of my zipper, and into the warmest place it could to relieve its self, damn! It's been a long time, she motioned me to come to the bed and I couldn't get there fast enough, I was turned on like I never been before, it was like she complete control of my body as well as my mind.

I thought you was going to cook me breakfast, I said sarcastically.

You don't see it on a plate for you, I walked in the door hot and ready, now hurry up and eat it before it gets cold!

I fell to my knees and went face first straight into her pussy, with my tongue out, taking long licks from her pussy to her ass for two reasons, one, being that I show her out of nowhere how she could become a buffet and the other reason being that I had to savior the taste and just like I thought, she tasted so fuckin good, my tongue danced on her clique like I was at a five star restaurant, I licked and sucked and licked and sucked, every drop of her cum that she released into my mouth, I was addicted, not just to the taste but to her actions as well, she grabbed my head making me keep my eyes open, as she slowly humped my face, telling me just what she expect of me, I knew after tonight I would be caught up in her, even possibly losing sleep, she was just for me, it was just that damn good, I couldn't take no more, I had to not only have her, but to give her what she was looking for, I got up on the bed while her legs was still in the air, and went as deep as my manhood would let me go inside her, her pussy wrapped around me like a blanket placed on a new born baby, pulled fresh from the wound. With every stroke I lost myself, more and more, it's crazy how I went from wanting her, to needing her in more ways than I could control, as she was humming all over me, I watch how I entered her in and out, the faces she made, made me believe I could be all that she needs and more. As we made love, I started to believe in a future, I was gone inside of her, in a matter of minutes, I lost everything, starting with my control, I couldn't pull out I busted all inside of her, after we was through I just laid with her and held her tight, from that night, we been together ever since, she was my best friend, I felt like I could tell her everything. Things got serious between us real quick and she got pregnant and ended up having my first child Aiden Wright, that was a day I could never forget, it was like my whole outlook on life changed, and all I wanted to do was be a better man for my son, I took a step back from the streets and tried to build the family that I never had, and shit got crazy real quick, Sarah found everything to argue with me about, which drove me to drink and do drugs like crazy, she stressed me out, I could understand it was her first child, so she didn't always know how to handle things. But she let her family interfere not only in our relationship but in every decision I involve myself in with my son. For my sake, I started to take a step back from Sarah but the more I stepped back the harder she made it for me to be a father to my son.

She put me on child support because I wanted out of the relationship, she put restraining orders on me for no reason so I couldn't see my son, telling the judge that I threaten her life, that hurt me the most because every since me and Sarah met, all I ever tried to do was love her and hold our family down, but she never listened to me, she put her friends before me, so there words mattered more and it's been killing me that she would even try to take my son away from me, she telling the judge I threaten her, poisoning the tree, I watered and worked so hard to grow all these years, it hurts because I thought I knew her, I thought her heart beat matched mine, and for once I found someone who completed me. My mind started to close in on me and all the love I had for her started draining out of my body, filling me with nothing but hate, she no longer mattered to me the way she used too, now when I see her, all I see is one more person that's in my way of being with my son, the hate built up drink after drink, then before I knew it I was doing lines of cocaine, women with they pussy out is running around my house everywhere, and the hard truth is I couldn't even get hard unless, I take care of my problem! But how! I don't know, no matter how much we fight, I still love her and plus I promised myself I wouldn't let my past be a part of my future. My mind wouldn't take a break, I thought about what she did to me all the time, day and night, until I make a judgment call, I could be stuck in these moments forever, so day after day I put thoughts together until I finally put the plan together, I had to make her look like an unfit mother, that's what the judge called me, because of my past, she called me a fuckin addict in front of everybody, even my kid, tearing me down anyway she could as if she never loved me at all, the more I thought and put my plan in place, the more I felt she deserved to lose her place in his world, not me, I let the power from the past take its place and before I knew it, I befriended her and got her hooked on coke and just like that, she was turned out real bad, I mean from selling pussy to robbing any and everybody She could for a couple of lines, this was only supposed to be just enough to dirty up her name for the courts, so I could get custody of my son back. But the problem is I can't fix what is broken, I went too far, I couldn't stand seeing her like this but also a part of me couldn't tell her no, the one time that I should have said no, she just kept calling me over and over again getting on my last nerve, she rushed me to pick up my son, she nag me because I didn't get up and fuck her this morning, she bugged me all day about bringing her some more coke, I rushed to the spot, grabbed the coke, rushed to her house so she would have something to get high with just so she would get the fuck off my back for a while. Damn I rushed, this is my fought, damn I shouldn't have rushed, this is my fought, my mind instantly went back to when we were happy, when we were in love, all she ever wanted me to do was be faithful to her but how could I tell her, that I fell in love with someone else, how could I tell her, I had two kids on her behind her back, I knew that news would of tore her apart. Now none of it matters anymore, as I look down at Sarah lifeless body, my heart was broken, I didn't mean for any of this to happen, when I rush into the house, I grabbed the wrong baggy, I grabbed the fentanyl, instead of the coke like I was supposed to. Now because of me Sarah is dead. I called the ambulance, they came and tried to revive her but she had been down for too long, so they couldn't bring her back, they ruled her death an overdose, from this day forward I will never be the same, nothing will ever be the same, I had won a battle over an enemy but lost my best friend in the process. Her death hurt the most not just because I was filled with regret but because I really didn't mean it. The courts awarded me full custody of my son, I prepared a beautiful funeral service for her, I felt like that's the least I could do, all of her family came along with mine to pay their final respects. I wanted to see her, everybody said she looked so beautiful, but my legs wouldn't let me stand to walk over and look at her, I couldn't stand to see her in a casket, as my son sat next to me, he never said a word, I watched the tears pour down his face as he looked at the casket, he was young but had a strong understanding between life and death, it hurt me to know he was hurting and that I'm the reason for his pain, I don't think I could ever tell him this, this is a secret I'm going to have to take to my grave. After the viewing of the body, we said a prayer, then the pastor asked if anybody would like to speak on her behalf, I stood up and made my way to the front, then out of nowhere I heard a loud scream.

Noooo! You motherfucker!

As I looked back, Sarah mother was coming towards me, she had her hand in her purse, moving at a fast paste.

You think you going to kill my baby and fuckin get away with it, she said as she was pulling her hand from her purse I could see the butt of the gun.

At that moment, my body lost its motion.

As she moved towards me, pulling the gun out ready to aim I stood my ground bracing for the shots I so deserved, out of nowhere a man rushed from his seat and fought her to the ground, wrestling the gun out of her hands, as shots fly around me, one to many times I came face to face with death, getting away by the skin of my teeth, after all this time, this life I put in front of me, after Sarah has been a mess, I turned around to go to the podium and my legs gave way. Not just my body was weak, my spirit and desire to live had checked out as well, Sarah truly mattered to me a lot, and her death hit me hard to the point I didn't know if I was going to recover, and at this point I really don't know if I even want to, when I got up to the podium, everyone's eyes was stuck on me, I went to open my mouth, looking to place words, farther then the eye can see, I pushed for the words to come out, but not one single word came to me. Damn, as I looked out into the crowd, a part of me wanted everybody to know, that I was sorry and if I could I would take it back, shit I would even die just to bring her back, I lost the only woman I truly loved, they needed to know that I meant that, but I pushed and pushed, still in hopes that words would flow out my mouth, but nothing came through, I was lost for words, what am I doing, knowing what I did, why was I even here in the first place, tears began to roll down my face and there is no paddle to coast the brake I turned around and walked away, it felt like when I looked out into that crowd, when they looked back, it was like they could stare into my soul, at this point I knew I had to be high as hell, or to be drunk and in pain to see or hear things clearly, I really just wanted to be alone or stuck with a thick bitch that suck good dick and don't talk, either way, I have to get far away from this place. For the next couple of weeks, my life got even more crazy with me drinking and drugging to kill the pain. All day my son cries for his momma, he walks around the house calling her name, looking in room after room, laying by the door, waiting for her to return, how do I tell him, that he might as well, give up, because his mother is gone and he never going to see her again. I know deep down that if I ever told him the truth he would hate me, I no longer looked at life the same, so I followed a few people advice and decide to go out and get some help. Now not too much worked, because it wasn't much I could open up about to the public and I wasn't good at telling these people my business but one psychiatrist chick told me, that if I can't say how I feel to anyone, then maybe I should at least try to write it all down in a journal and I did, I put my every emotional thought or feeling I ever had in that book, shit I mean things I knew would probably get me a hundred years if they ever found it. On the front of the journal I wrote my dirty little secrets and I put it away in a safe where nobody would be able to find it.

The more I did the excise, the more I was starting to feel like things were getting back to normal. Slowly but surely, things were starting to improve when it came to the relationship between me and my son Aiden, we started building a lot of good memories together, locking away the old, and over time I taught him everything i know. He is the mirror to my image, I just have to be the father to him that I never had, I broke the game down to him step by step, the same way May-so broke the game down to me. All I know is I will never let my son do what I did or let him go through what I been through, for him I only want the best, time was flying and he was growing up on me real quick, I could tell that he had over time developed a strong mind of his own.

In the words of Aiden:

I feel like shit started fucking up for me in life at birth, I was blessed to have my mom in my life foe a little while, then puff she was gone just like that. I lost her to drugs, her love for them was more then she had for me, if she would have just loved me more, then she would be here with me. Over the years my dad taught me everything I know about life, he took good care of me, now the tables have turned. Everyday my father lives in an unspeakable pain, he barely eats or sleeps and he drinks all the time, as a matter of fact, he is what you call a true fish to the water.

And I wish I could take all his pain away and get him back to the person I need him to be, I know together, me and my dad can take this world over, can't nobody fuck with him when he on point, but over these last couple of years my dad has been just falling apart. I been having to carry the load and it's cool I don't mind taking care of him, but I have to admit, taking care of him is far from an easy job! He is no open book, the man is very secretive and it just makes me wonder just what type of secrets is he holding on too. I mean, me and my dad use to talk about everything growing up over the years, I feel I have to be the holder of his secrets, I just have to some way, get my dad to let me in! I know this won't be easy, he always told me never to trust a soul and I keep my eyes open. Sometimes I caught my dad having conversations with my mom as if she were right in the room with him, I just hope I could figure out what's on his mind before he loses it and ends up in the crazy house or something and from the looks of it, I'm running out of time by him talking to the dead shows me that either the love he had for my mom was real or shit getting real ugly, to get a head start on things I figured I go talk to a couple of my dad's old friends to see, if I could find out a little bit about his past and weeks of searching my dad past life I ran across a guy named Mike-D and he ain't tell me shit but that he use to run up under some old dude, they use to think he was his dad, he said he go by the name of May-so, and that he been in the same spot for years, I didn't waste no time, I got the address and went to go pay May-so a Lil visit. When I got there, first I knocked on the door, it sounded like I heard movement coming from inside so I decided to move closer so I could put my ear to the door, then just like that, someone stepped behind me, instantly I felt out of place, in my mind I could hear my dad say, boy keep your eye on the prize.

What the fuck you want Lil nigga? He said as I go to turn around I saw an old man standing there with a long ass chrome 38 special pointed at my head.

I! I! I! want to speak to a guy named May-so!

Lol wrong fuckin answer! He said as he cooked the barrel, grabbing my throat, applying pressure to his grip.

What the fuck you want with May-so? I ain't been fuckin these Lil young hoes around here so who the fuck is you? And hurry up because shit about to get messy son!

I could tell by the look in his eyes, he meant every word that he said. I'm Lamar Wright son!

He searched my eyes for my soul and he also gave me the feeling, that if he seen the wrong one behind these eyes, he would take it.

And why are you here son?

I just want to ask you some questions about my dad!

He lowered his gun, looked to his left then his right, then raised it again, put your fuckin hands up!

He checked me all over for weapons, which I had none and thank God, because if I did, it ain't no telling what would of happen next.

What is it you want to know?

Excuse my language, but what's got my dad head so fucked up?

May-so gave me a look, like that question was the switch which a drain his soul, I almost instantly started to apologlze, shit was deeper than I thought, and I couldn't just leave empty handed I had to know!

Your dad grew up in the streets, but he always longed for love, the type of love only a father could give to his son, he looked for it, in any and every place he could find it and believe it or not, that shit got him hurt over and over again.

Yeah! I could tell.

Hell yeah! The closest to love he got was the relationship he had with your mother, though I think he had another woman with two kids, you know you got a brother and a sister don't you?

No! and my dad never cheated on my mom!

May-so cut his eye to the lack of knowledge the Lil boy had, he been picking for his own personal information, opening his eyes to what he now knows as true in return giving the Lil dude what he wanted to keep him going, without him knowing he was getting everything he needed. Then just like he did with his dad, he decided to give him some game, he felt like he was his grand baby, he couldn't just send him home empty handed.

You know what Lil Wright? I'm Aiden!

Ok! I think your granddad can probably give you some better input on your dad's life, since he is the reason your dad is so fucked up!

Why would you say that? Aiden said as he leaned in to learn more.

I'm just gone write down the address, I'm pretty sure he gone answer all ;vour questions, all right!

Yes, sir, and thanks for this.

No don't thank me for this one young, just giving you what you want, I'm glad I could be of service.

Yes, yes, yes, I do, I got a lot of questions I got to ask him.

May-so walked Lil Aiden to the door, let him out and locked it behind him.

Damn now I have a lead I can chase, plus I can meet my granddad and he can give me the run down about everything.

He didn't waste no time, he headed to his granddad house, he had to know, what his granddad would tell him about his dad.

Hello, hello, Lamar said as he answered the phone. Your son is going to see your dad!

What! May-so! What is you talking about?

That mafuckin son of yours, shola is a talker, places in life I thought we were better then, but I guess not and I raised you! Who would have thought it would have been you saying fuck me too!

May-so what is you talking about I never fuckin crossed you!

You killed my grandbaby, I should have shot his Lil ass in the face, yeah we were alone! What the fuck is you on May-so? I didn't kill your grandbaby you tripping.

Cassie motherfucker, huh, you didn't kill Cassie you bitch ass nigga, go right ahead and lie to me!

Ole shit! I never knew that Cassie was May-so grandbaby and that he been on my ass for doing it the whole time, May-so was one person I could not lie too, he would read right through it, if I even tried, so many questions ran through my head, how did my son even know who May-so was and why was he poking around, what was he looking to find?

Ole what the fuckin cat got your tongue, you ain't got to say nothing, I did my homework, I know what's up! You took something from me that was so precious, and Lamar I could have just done the same, my heart wouldn't let me, my mafuckin heart, it wouldn't! but I know his real granddad is gone have a field day with his Lil ass!

May-so come on man! When did he leave? This morning around 9:00am.

I searched for a clock around the room, until I spotted one on the wall, it said 1:30pm. What the fuck!

Although you might be too late, look at it this way, I didn't even have to fuckin call at all, he probably getting rid of that Lil mafucka body right now as we speak!

He began to laugh in my ear, and I ain't gone lie it sent a chill up my spine, I could picture some of the things my dad a do, shit he shot me.

May-so what's the address?

Yeah! You can have the address, just make sure you kill that son of a bitch for my grandbaby Aiden, May-so said as he laughed into my ear once more then he hung up.

As quick as he gave me the address the quicker I was on my way to my dad's house. Aiden:

I had finally arrived at my granddad house, I ran up to the door, and knocked hard three times, no answer, I began to beat on the door out of control, refusing to believe that I'm in the wrong place, I stood my ground unto someone can come to the door and give me the answers to what I was looking for.

A man rushed to the door, and snatched it open.

Who the fuck is you Lil dude? He said as he stared me up and down. Damn granddad you don't recognize your own grandbaby?

Grandbaby! The thoughts ran in the back of his head, ok yes, I did say I was going to baby sit for a while, for my daughter Nay-Nay.

A boy where is your momma? She gone!

He gave him a look like he wanted to kick his ass for having a smart mouth, not knowing every word he spoke about his mom was in truth, they watched the basketball game, barely sharing a word, it took Aiden to break the silence before the conversation could get in motion.

Granddad I got a couple questions I want to ask you about.

Dude that shit got to wait till after the game, just chill with all the questions right now alright! Out of nowhere the phone rung, then granddad mode changed.

Hello what's up!

Dad I'm on my way to drop Kevin off to you so y'all can finally spend some time together.

Instantly a confusion started to fill his mind, if she had not dropped his grandson off yet, then who the fuck has he been sitting with all this time.

Nay-Nay quit playing!

Daddy I'm not playing I'm on my way, just have to run a couple places first then we will be right over.

It's cool baby, go ahead and take your time, I'm about to get up and do some cleaning up real quick!

Ok daddy love you.

Love you too baby!

It was like the boy could feel the energy come into the room, so he got up and started heading for the door.

And where the luck do you think your going?

I have to get home before my dad notices I'm gone.

Your dad! Who is your dad? Listen boy you touch that door, and I'm going to pop your ass in the back of your head and bury you in the backyard, so don't make another move.

The cock of the gun stopped Aiden in his tracks, heart racing, not knowing what to do next. Who the fuck is your dad boy, I ain't gone ask you again!

Lamar! Lamar Wright!

O yeah! Get the fuck out of here! What do I owe for this visit, and why would he send you to die at this early age? I thought he would have told your ass I tried to kill his Lil bitch ass, when he was little.

Why!

Let's just say I don't fuck with this side of the family! You said you tried to kill him, what did you do to him?

The same thing I'm about to do to you, but I'm gone finish the job this time! Pop! Pop, pop! Pop, pop, pop!

I heard the shots and my legs lost all strength they had in them, damn this was it, I passed out, damn is this how I'm going to die.

As soon as the body dropped I stood over him, begging for him to move, so I could deliver a shit load more into his body, no regrets just a big relief off my shoulders, I stepped over his body to get to my son, he had passed out after he heard the shots, I picked him up and took him home.

Aiden:

As I started to come to, I remembered everything up until I fainted, I felt all over my body in a panic to see if I had been shot. I heard the shots! I know I was hit, damn where am I, I knew I was not in a hospital, I was in fear I might have crossed over to the other side, I began to fight for answers, the first face that came into my sight was my dad's.

What's going on! How did I get here? I said to my dad in a panic trying my best to get up. Chill! Relax, don't worry about it son, everything's alright.

What! Was I dreaming, this had to be a bad dream!

No, son it wasn't a dream, son, answer this question for me, he said with a look of deep concern on his face.

What's up dad?

What the fuck have you been looking for? I keep hearing how you been playing detective around town, trying to look into my past! What is it that you want to know?

Everything! I said as I searched his eyes for the truth that's been missing between us.

Son, there is no one person on this earth that knows everything about me, the only one who knows me through and through is God and that's the way I would like to keep it! And if you want to know everything, he will be the only one who can give you that information, other than that chill with that shit, if you want to know something about me and if it's in my power to tell you I will, but never forget I love you.

Up until this moment everything had been real tough between us, no real emotion being shown, not that much love shown at all, but once I heard him say I love you, for the ftrst time in a long time I knew in my heart that he meant it. That day made us closer, stuck together like glue, truly being each other strength, but I would be lying if I didn't tell you dad don't slip, every now and then, one minute he's up happy and moving around sniiling, writing in some damn notebook, that he never lets me see or read, which only makes me wonder what does he about in that thing, probably all the hidden property's and money he got hid everywhere, or it could tell about all those secrets he won't tell me about, either way I get the chance I'm going to read that book and the next time he gets drunk, might be my shot, when he gets to many drinks in him he gets messy, and I do mean messy to the point he forgets some of the things he says or does. Over time my dad taught everything he knew about the business, taught me the ropes about the street code, how to move and move money around in case I was ever in trouble. He has called me out on all my weaknesses, pushed me to limits I didn't know I had and here he is being over powered by his weakness, how could you teach a person to walk a walk that you're not even walking yourself?

as I look at him, I could hear him say, strength is what rules the jungle over and over again like a broken record, the way I see it is if he keeps this up he won't be in power for long.

Lamar:

Time has been flying by, it seems like ages since Sarah has been gone but I still miss her. I been building with my son, trying to give him and my other two kids the love they need a long with the game from the streets, I always feel like I'm running out of time so I'm hard on them at times trying to make sure that they really get the lessons that I'm teaching them, I just know I'm not going to always be here forever, another thing that's been killing me is bringing them all together, it's just never the right time to tell Aiden about his brother and sister but it has to happen, this has been another secret of mines that needs to come out, my moods been up and down, going through changes like a bitch, I keep fighting myself over Sarah death, one minute, then the next minute, I'm writing in my journal strengthening myself, trying to better myself in my recovery. It's hard trying to better myself for my son without living out my pain in the open. I don't know where to start or if I will ever truly heal, one minute it feels like me and my son is getting closer, then the next minute, there feels like a big distance between us, and he's getting older so I try to give him his space, but that's about to change every day I don't confess to him about what happen to his mom, I feel like nothing more than a liar and a part of me dies inside, I really didn't mean it, this time it really was a mistake.

Aiden:

The time has finally come, where I could read that damn book my dad had been hiding away. It's a moment of my truth that I been looking for, I'll start from the beginning, and won't stop until it's reached its end. what caught my eye was what were on the cover of the journal (my dirty little secrets) once I began to start reading I seen it was a true open book to my dad's inner most thoughts, every emotion and moment he had in life he actually put in this book, even shit that was held personal for him and what's personal to him became personal to me. I know I could show him I could keep his secrets; shit I could be the one to hold him down. I'll even go as far as kill them mafucka's who hurt my dad if I could see him smile again, but I ain't gone lie, my dad fucked my head up with the story about my granddad, how he shot him and the way he shot him, got me scared to let anybody sit behind me, and I ain't never giving nobody my gun either, fuck that! As I sit and think about everything I could have easily lost my life not knowing how my granddad felt about us, if I would of knew that shit I would of never went to his house to talk, I would of went there to put a bullet in his brain. Damn this all sounds crazy to me, how could he treat family this way, that mafucka almost had me, I can't slip like that evsr again. As soon as I opened the book, it started talking about murders he committed when he was just a child. I couldn't believe it, it talked about his darkest and deepest secrets that nobody should of knew, why would he write this down for anybody to see, I cried on a couple, especially Cassie, she didn't have to die. My dad is truly a monster, and what scared me is it couldn't be seen through the incident face I knew. a part of me wanted to stop but I just couldn't, I had to read more, I wondered did it say anything about my mom, I know they had their up's and down but I also knew that he loved her with all his heart. Then I came across some lady by the name of Miona, my dad talked so sweet about her, like they was in love, like they had been fucking around for a while, I wondered was this what May-so was trying to tell me, then pieces about my mom began to fall into the story, my whole body begin to overheat, I became so filled with rage, I couldn't stop shaking, I never knew all the pain my dad took my mom through, he introduced her to drugs, and here I was thinking she just choose drugs over me, the more I read, the more I began to get sick to my stomach, I just couldn't believe what I was reading and then, the next part of the story broke my heart, it was right here in my dad's hand writing, my momma didn't just die from doing drugs, my dad killed her, he took my momma away from me! The tears began to fall down my face uncontrollably, my dad wrote this shit! Murder after murder in detail, and look what I found, damn I can't even question his path because I knew it already, I just knew it was something that he was holding back from me. Thought after thought took over my brain, I didn't want to stand I didn't want to sit, I needed some answers and I needed them now! Damn! Why didn't he tell me? I have to get out of here, I just wanted to hurt something or somebody the way my dad hurt me. I got up and put the book back in its place, I had enough I didn't want to read no more, I just knew I couldn't be here when my father gets back because of how I feel right now, there ain't no telling what I would do. Before I left, I looked for all the information I could find on Miona, address, place of business, anything I could find, I had to find her, she was the main reason my family had got tore apart, I didn't waste no time, as I pulled up to her house, I watched my surroundings for about an hour, then she came into my view, I watched her from outside her window get undressed take a shower and then get dressed again, she has an amazing body, tight little waist, thick thighs I could fall sleep between and a fat ole ass to go with it, real pretty long hair and the face of a baby doll. I could see what my dad seen in her, but fuck that! She got some questions to answer, I want to know did she know he had a family and she is the reason everything has fallen apart. I stepped outside the car and headed to the back door of the house, I checked the door knob and to my surprise, the back door was open, I slipped inside, I let my eyes Rome around the room, I had to check my surroundings, gun next to my hip, if anybody jump out of place, I'm killing them with no hesitation!

Miona:

Today has been a long day for me, I just want to take a shower and go to bed, when the water from the shower touched my body I felt a deep comfort come over my body, I been thinking about Lamar really hard lately, it gets that really bad sometimes and I get to checking for him, damn, that's my baby, in so many places I could feel him, he truly has my heart, even dough I know his heart is with another. It's been a minute since I had him inside of me and I can't lie, there are times I fiend for him, especially when shit is bad and its bad right now! I'm horny as hell and I don't want nobody else but him as crazy as it seems he's my family, we have a family, people tell me to move on but I can't, I even leave the back door open for him, just in case he might want to come home one day. Sometimes he makes me feel like a Sucka, but i love him and you just can't help who you love. I hate when I lose myself, shaking my head I cut the shower off, and watch the water go down the drain wishing I could go with it, then I dried off, I know I have to get out of my head, its only that way every time I think about Lamar, that I get off focus. As I put my lotion on I imagine sucking his dick and getting ready to get my walls tore down, which is the key right now, I picked up the phone,

I wondered would he answer. We haven't been in a good place lately everything has just been about the kids. Even dough I want Lamar, it's a chance he might not come! Damn I have to try I really need this shit fixed right now, it's been a while, I wish I could call somebody (fuck)! Then I heard a sound, it sounds like somebody is coming up the stars right now, damn I thought about Lamar that hard that he could feel my connection, I rushed out the bathroom door to meet him. I couldn't wait to wrap my arms around him and tell him how I been feeling all this time, I really want us to get back together.

Hoping that this could turn out to be a good night after all, as I came down the stairs, I ran into an unknown figure, fuck my reaction was to put everything I had in reverse.

Uh uh bitch don't do that!

What! Who the fuck is you? And what the fuck do you want? Miona said as fear filled her eyes trying her best to get away.

I want a life for a life! I lose my momma in this game, you and my daddy played, so yea, how about a life for a life!

She adjusted her eyes to his face, Aiden is that you?

Don't act like you know me bitch! Aiden said, as the closer he got, the angrier he got. Aiden where is your dad? And what the fuck do you want?

His intentions went from talking to murder in beyond seconds, a rage came over him he couldn't control, he rushed her, meeting her in the middle of the stairs. Once he reached her he punched her in the face with an over hand right, dropping her where she stood.

Miona:

What the fuck! I tried my best to get back up the stairs, but my legs wouldn't move as fast as my brain, if only I could get to my room, then I could get to my gun! Oh my God! What's going on? Where are my kids? Will he hurt my kids? Fuck! I got to get to my gun, then barn! He rushed me and punched me in my face, over and over again, each punch that was delivered was harder than the last, and he didn't stop until I passed out. When I woke up, he was fucking me, laying all his weight on top of me, pounding me, there was a blank look in his eyes, his heart was cold, oh my Ood, this motherfucker is going to kill me! Blood filled my eyes, so it was hard for me to see, but I couldn't just lay here and let him do this, so I fought with all I had in me.

Aiden:

The more she fought, the more turned on I got, I could tell her pussy loved me with every stroke, I choked her and beat her, she kept squirting all over my dick, damn she made it easy to fall in love, I would choke her just up to the point she was about to pass out, then I would let her go, watching which choice she would make next, the choice to fight me or to breathe, one time I even went too far, so I had to give her mouth to mouth to bring her back, and when I wasn't giving her mouth to mouth I would violently fuck her throat, which made me laugh because she threw up all over me, I moaned a little, everything was wet, oh fuck yeah, I love it! I could see I was knocking the fight right out of her, because every time she tried, I would press the 40 Cal to her temple, just to remind her who was in control, I bet you she thought about just how precious life truly is. I could feel myself about to cum, I grab a hold of her hair, and beat her throat, with my dick, like it was a pussy, while I looked deeply into her eyes, I could see it in her eyes, defeat, she would never be the same after this, so right after I came.

Pop! pop! pop! pop! pop!

Our business was finish, I got to work, after I cut off her head, I went outside and broke down a car battery so I could throw the battery acid on her pussy to try to kill the evidence, before I took those steps I tasted her sweet pussy for the last time, dead or not I didn't give a fuck! I got everything I wanted, a life for a life! The rest will be left to the highest, I r'elt a strong relief when I left out the door. I took her head with me, so I could bury it with my thoughts.

Lamar:

I haven't seen or heard from Aiden in days now, and that ain't like him, we usually talk every day, I called Miona phone back after she called me and didn't answer either, I called her what had to had been a hundred times, and she still didn't answer or shoot me a text, she has never been that mad at me when she didn't answer the phone. It's been a lot of weird shit going on, then out of nowhere I got a phone call from an unknown number, at first, I wasn't going to answer, but something just kept driving me to answer the call, it came with a funny feeling in my stomach so I did, it was my babies Myona and Jyei on the phone screaming and crying, they found there mother murdered, the news hit me hard and hurt me bad, when they told me how they found her, I got sick to my stomach, damn was this my karma coming back to haunt me for all the shit I did in the past? All I know is now I have to step it up and let Aiden know about his brother and sister, I hate I have to throw this on him but he has to know. I searched all around town for him, blowing his phone up beginning to worry, he didn't answer not once! All I could think about is how I hoped he didn't go on a stupid ass mission that could of got his ass fucked up, I know the streets is a jungle I can't save him all the time, but I got to at least try to look out for him, just like my others, even dough I was hurting bad my kids need me I can't check out now, I'm all they got, I got tired ofjust riding around so I just decided to go home, I know Aiden is going to pop up sooner or later, I pulled up to the house and low and behold, Aiden was coming out of the house, with a bag, moving fast like he was in a rush, I jumped out the car to approach him and he threw me the cold shoulder, I could tell something was bothering him, to the point he couldn't even make eye contact, I pushed for conversation.

Aiden! Son come here I have to talk to you, this is very important!

Not right now dad! I had a long day and I just really want to be left alone, I just want to clear my head, Aiden said as the anger began to build in his chest it was hard to even look at his dad.

Even dough he heard his sons every word, he pushed anyway because he had so much to get off his chest in so little time, he will be meeting his brother and sister in a matter of hours, things was about to get real crazy between him and his family, over the years it's been a lot going on, it's time for us to start over, do everything the right way.

Naw son I can't wait another minute son, this can't wait! Aiden:

As I looked into my dad face, he looks like something was off, he was speaking different, looking off, moving different, and kept pushing to talk to me and about what I don't know, all I know is I'm just so fuckin angry right now, how could he do what he did to my mom? I just don't think I could stand talking to him about anything, so I moved pass him, I opened the car door and got into the driver seat, as soon as I entered, my dad opened the door to the back seat and sat directly behind me, which is weird because there is no one but me in the front. My mind instantly begins to Tace and a million questions begin to flow through my brain, the first one being, I wonder do he know what I did?

Lamar:

Son I got to holla at you shit! If you leaving then I got to ride with you I said as I slipped into the back seat, a real sharp pain shot up my back, I still could feel the pain from when my dad shot me, that's one of the things I carry every day, I leaned over to try to relieve the pain, I sat up a little so I could catch an eye sight with him to let him know, we really got to talk and this is serious!

Aiden:

Damn what the fuck is he doing sitting behind me? I begin to get real uncomfortable, every time I check the rearview, we lock eyes, I could tell shit was getting weird between us, he had something on his mind.

Dad what's up man, why don't you come sit in the front seat? Son I'm cool! I just got to lay down.

My mind is racing, I know this mafucka ain't about to try and kill me over no bitch or did he find out that I seen his little secrets he was hiding! Then out of nowhere he popped the question.

Aiden! Do you have your gun on you?

It was the same question, his dad asked him before he shot him! Damn, this is it, he can try to take my life in any moment. I shot the question back at him to see if he would connect the dots, I wanted him to know I know so it won't be no surprise!

Lamar:

I had asked to see his gun, I had beef on the side of town we were headed too, May-so spot and I know that wasn't the place he was going but I had to be sure, Aiden got a weird look in his eye, like something is bothering him, we got to talk before shit gets out of hand!

Dad why you need my gun? You know you good with me right, he said as he searched my eyes for an answer.

I didn't have an answer for him, how could I tell him I didn't trust him. Aiden:

I shot that question out loud and clear and my father still didn't catch the mood, instead he insisted I give it to him, so I pulled over.

After Aiden pulled over I sat up a little more so I would be able to reach for the gun, I also knew things could get emotional between us, I'm putting everything on the table, Miona and the kids, the death of his mom, all I can do is hope that he can forgive me, I love him and I really didn't mean it, as I leaned in, all of a sudden!

Pop! Pop!

And just like that my chest was on fire!

You want my gun? You fuckin want the gun dad! You thought you was gone do me like your dad did you huh! Answer me! Huh?

For, for, forgive me, Lamar said as he fought like hell to breathe, he could feel his body taking in to the stress. Damn I got some much to say, he fought to get out the words as Aiden opened the door and walked towards him. Your bro, brother and sis, sister, for, forgive me!

Aiden:

After I turn and unloaded my gun into my dad chest I hurried up and jumped out the car before he got a shot off, after I didn't see any fast movement I opened the door, to finish the job, as he fought for words, it tore me apart to look into his eyes, but I had too.

Dad I love you, you take care, this is my show now!

Pow!

The shot hit him square between the eyes, I took out my phone snapped the picture, then made the call.

Ring, ring, ring, Hello!

May-so, Aiden said as he answered the phone. Yeah what's up?

It's done!

I need da heart, I lost mine, you hear me, get that for me and bring it to me and we good! Yes, sir.

Then we hung up.

May-so:

May-so laid back in the chair and a slight grin came across his face as the picture of Lamar Wright came across the screen of his phone, chest wide open and a hole in his head, Aiden is going to bring him to me, a heart for a heart, when he killed

Cassie he killed me, I feel like a dead man walking, a body with no soul, since she been gone, now I want to cut out his heart and jar it, I'm even gone leave it in the living room for everyone to see, fuck'em! I would have killed his son, but in truth, he was a victim too, I knew his dad had not told him the truth about his mom, if he would have, I would not have been able to break their bond! When I told him about his mom, I knew he wouldn't believe me, so I gave him the direction to the journal, not what was in it but I knew I could spark his interest, and from it, the truth would come out, I set everything up even Aiden going to his granddad's house, I knew if I called, he would come running to save his precious boy, I played him against his fears and turned what he loved the most against him.

Because that was his only true weakness, the love of his kids, a mistake any real father would make in this world.

Aiden:

As soon as I got off the phone I jumped in the car to head towards May-so, I need to hurry up and get his body over there, he wants the heart or something! And then we gone place him off in this car somewhere and burn it, can't risk nothing. See I took the money three other mafucka's had on his head, plus May-so, then i could hit his safe, all six of them, so I'm gone be straight on the bread, dad would be proud of me right now for stepping into my true man hood, I could see him now he would smile and say son, you growing up on me! I can't fake it, I'm gone miss my dad, when I killed him, I lost a lot and thought it would be a life for a life, but when it came to my mom I had to have two! If only he would have told me what happen, he would still be here today. I paid for the funeral and stayed at a distance, May-so attended the service, there I handed him my dad journal, it explained in detail what happen to his grandbaby Cassie, I knew he was dying to know, it's only right, he brought me to the truth, so I brought him his, dough some truth doesn't set you free, word is right after the funeral May-so couldn't live with the pain so he ended up taking his own life, I seen my great grandma Vickie with two little kids, I only wondered, who they were, one of the safes had a will, that my dad left and it had three names on it Aiden, Jye1, and Myona, the Myona name is spelled close to Miona! I know he wasn't about to leave that bitch no money, he laughed it off as he walked out the door to the funeral home never looking back, there was only room to move forward.

TATE BLU
BE